Alligator Stew

Tales from Delbert, Arkansas

By CD Mitchell

Southern Yellow Pine
Publishing

Published by;
Southern Yellow Pine (SYP) Publishing
4351 Natural Bridge Rd.
Tallahassee, FL 32305

www.syppublishing.com

This is a work of fiction. Names, characters, places, and events that occur either are
the products of the author's imagination or are used fictitiously. Any resemblance to
actual persons, places, or events is purely co-incidental.
The contents and opinions expressed in this book do not necessarily reflect the
views and opinions of Southern Yellow Pine Publishing, nor does the mention of
brands or trade names constitute endorsement.

ISBN-10: 1940869056
ISBN-13: 978-1-940869-05-6

Author Photo: CD Mitchell
Cover Design: Taylor Nelson

Printed in the United States of America
First Edition
January 2014

Acknowledgements

"Good Intentions" appears as "Additions or Substitutions" in the *Arkansas Literary Forum*, Fall 2006, and in *Tartt's Anthology III: Incisive Fiction from Emerging Writers* published by Livingston Press.

"Alligator Stew" was selected by guest editor John Dufresne for inclusion in the inaugural issue of *Real South.*

"Goat and Dumplins" appeared in the inaugural issue of *The Unbound Press*, Spring 2007.

"The Sheriff of Jester County" appears in the Spring 2009 issue of *Natural Bridge*.

"Poverty Line" appears in the September 2013 issue of *The Writing Disorder.*

"The Mayor of Delbert, Arkansas" appears in Volume XX of *The Evansville Review.*

"Penumbra" appears in *Bear Catz Claw*

"Ferdinand C. Posey" appears in Volume 7.1 of *Big Muddy*.

Dedication

Thank you to Southern Yellow Pine Publishing for making this book a reality. I also want to thank Mary Jane Ryals for revision suggestions she made for "Poverty Line," Cary Holladay for revision suggestions she made for "The Mayor of Delbert, Arkansas," and Silas House for revision suggestions he was kind enough to make in a rejection notice for "The Sheriff of Jester County." In the first story I work-shopped at McNeese State University, Neil Connelly suggested I was trying to make my stories do far too much. He believed I had enough material in that story for a whole collection. He was wrong. I made two collections from that story. Thank you, all.

Contents

Introduction

In the summer of 1990, Iben Browning predicted an apocalyptic earthquake would strike the New Madrid Fault on December 3rd, 1990, devastating the heartland from St. Louis to Memphis. After the San Andreas, the New Madrid Fault line is the most active earthquake zone in the United States. The fault has produced devastating earthquakes in the past, and scientists agree it is simply a matter of time before the next one occurs.

I lived through this experience, and I vividly remember the school closings, the businesses that shuttered up for the day, the rush to buy bottled water, canned Spam, batteries, gasoline, and bullets. I also remember the day after when everyone forgot about the earthquake as if the threat had never existed. This seemed even more insane than the rush of preparations that preceded December 3rd.

While in graduate school in Lake Charles, I worked at a Sears store selling lawn and garden items. During one week we had the threat of two hurricanes. We sold over 200 generators. A week later, after both hurricanes had curved and missed Lake Charles, nearly 200 generators were returned. That week I recognized a pattern that has fascinated me ever since.

The tales in *Alligator Stew* reveal the fictional lives and actions of the people who lived through the Iben Browning prediction.

In Delbert, Arkansas, the people felt other things were more important than a pending apocalypse, like Wink Gaskill's beer permit application for his new convenience store. "If we allow him to sell beer here, next thing you know we'll have crack houses, whore houses and casinos on every street corner."

Some of the town-folks feared the success of Browning's earlier predictions. He had predicted the eruption of Mount St. Helens, and was rumored to have predicted the San Francisco earthquake that interrupted the World Series. But when the day came and went, people chose to discount the prediction and the threat. "I

1

guess only Jesus Christ himself could have gotten it right two times in a row."

In this story collection the townspeople barrel towards their date with destiny while dealing with infidelity, lust, sexual and domestic abuse, drug addiction, cancer, family histories, bigotry, murder, ambition, mental illness, loss, failure, mistakes, local gossip, elections, and professional wrestling.

In spite of Iben Browning's prediction of an apocalyptic earthquake, December 3rd, 1990, came and went without incident. And, as with all other predictions of apocalypse, the town folks breathed a collective sigh of relief and went about returning their generators to Sears for a refund, pouring their cache of gasoline into their trucks and ATV's, and dumping stored gallons of water on their lawns.

They went back to dealing with the everyday problems that make a foretold disaster seem small in comparison. Facing a once in a lifetime predicted apocalypse, the residents of Delbert, Arkansas, prove that the truly apocalyptic events are the ones they face every day.

Good Intentions

Archie Snell walked into Campbell's Café and eased over to the east corner. The windows there looked out upon the street, and every Friday for the last five years he sat at the same table. The Marmon Plant where he welded the racks that held the clothes in the Walmart stores worked a four-day, ten-hour shift that gave him Fridays off, unless he worked overtime. There had been no overtime since Melissa died in 1985. Five years later Archie still missed his wife, but as he sat, he watched for Jenny Wilkinson, his waitress.

Jenny never dressed up, and he knew as a single mother of twins, she struggled to survive. Archie wanted to ask Jenny to the Gillette Coon Supper last January, but he was afraid the biggest political event in the state of Arkansas might have been too intimidating for a first date. He thought about buying her a dress for the event and even found one at the Belk's store over in Success. There were no longer any nice dress shops in downtown Delbert, and although Archie was no expert on fashion, he knew he had to go somewhere else to buy anything nice. Made of purple silk, the dress would cling to every curve of her tiny body, but Archie worried the low-cut neckline would reveal too much of her ample breasts – too much for Jenny. Archie saw how hard Jenny worked at the café, how she struggled to maintain her independence. He didn't want to offend her with the dress—a man can have the best intentions and still offend a woman for reasons he could never suspect—so he went to the supper alone. The dress still hung from its mannequin the last time he drove by Belk's.

The café bristled with the sounds of loud conversation and shouted orders of food. Archie saw Jenny look his way and smile. Leaving a dollar tip, whether he had a meal or a cup of coffee, always made Jenny smile, but he hoped that wasn't the only reason she was glad to see him.

A dwindling community with a small city square, Delbert, Arkansas, hadn't changed much in decades, and the changes had been more of subtraction than addition. The old courthouse sat empty now;

3

condemned by the State when the legislature passed new earthquake standards for government buildings near the New Madrid Fault Line. By 1989, all the government offices had moved to a modern, earthquake proof building in Success, the new county seat. The dedication of the new courthouse and the Vietnam Veterans Memorial honoring the five boys the county lost overseas drew the biggest crowd since the county fair.

Then Iben Browning, a California Seismologist, predicted a devastating earthquake would hit the New Madrid Fault on December 3rd, 1990. April was upon them, and the city only had seven more months to prepare. Browning had predicted the exact day of the earthquake that hit San Francisco on October 17th of 1989—the earthquake that interrupted the World Series between the Giants and Athletics and injured thousands of people. He had also predicted the Mt. St. Helens eruption. The joke at Campbell's Café was that he'd correctly predicted the groundhog would see its shadow on Groundhog Day. But Delbert sat five miles from the geographical center of the New Madrid Fault line, and the threat of a major earthquake was real.

On the east side of the cafeteria, a poster pinned to the wall interrupted the lines of antique phones that circled the dining area. Yellowed from time and cigarette smoke, the sign described the breakfast special: "2 Eggs, Choice of Meat (ham, sausage or bacon), Biscuits and Gravy or Toast, with Hash Browns and Coffee: $2.99, plus tax." At the very bottom of the poster, in even bigger letters, the sign said "No Substitutions, Just Omissions." A distant relative and namesake of the singer from Delight, Arkansas, Glen Campbell owned Campbell's Cafe. He also served as the head cook. Glen collected old telephones, and the antiques lined the walls of the dining area.

Jenny walked over to Archie, bringing him a cup of coffee. In a voice small enough to match her petite frame she said, "The usual?"

"How are your angels doing? They ready for Easter?"

"I start talking about my girls and you won't ever get your breakfast, Archie." Thirteen year-old, green-eyed twins, Jenny's girls dreamed of growing up to be gypsies. They had convinced most of the boys in Delbert they already knew how to cast a spell after showing

4

up at school last month with a worn voodoo book their mother bought them at the Nu-2-U Flea Market. The flea market occupied the space vacated by Belk's after the store had moved to Success.

"Let me see a menu."

"Our breakfast menu hasn't changed since Glen put that poster up last year. What do you want, a Danish?"

"I been ordering the same thing in here for five years. Just thought I'd try something different."

"Glen's supposed to be learning how to cook omelets at some cooking school in Little Rock this weekend. You can order one of them next Friday. But I'll have him scramble your eggs and put a slice of cheese on them for now." She wrote on her little order book.

"That's a substitution," Archie said.

"No, that's an addition. Cost you a quarter extra."

"Then I want fries instead of hash browns."

"Now, that's a substitution. 'Can't do it." She turned away, then stopped and looked back at Archie. "What's gotten into you this morning? You never order anything different." Then she smiled and walked away.

Archie and Melissa had celebrated ten years of marriage on their last anniversary together in 1985. They married on Ground Hog Day, and Melissa had laughed and said that she would forever be Archie's shadow.

"No matter where you go, I'll be there with you," she told him.

They lived a simple life together, a typical Delbert family working two jobs; Archie at the Marmon plant welding store fixtures, and Melissa as a secretary at the White Law Firm. They survived on their good credit, with the bulk of their paychecks going toward their mortgage, car payments and insurance. Once a month, if they'd had no other surprise expenses, they splurged for dinner at Ed's Catfish House at Success, where Melissa would eat her fill of crab-legs off the buffet. But Melissa had missed a lot of work in 1985, and not only had they stopped the monthly outing to Ed's, they'd used all of their tax refund to catch up their bills. Melissa suffered from debilitating headaches, and the missed work had strained their limited budget—and their relationship.

"You only have headaches when I want sex or when you have to go to work," he'd said their last morning together.

"Archie, that's just not so."

"Why don't you go see the doctor?"

"With what? We can't even make the co-pay for an office call. It's all we can do to keep seeing that marriage counselor."

"We could if you'd get out of bed and go to work every day," Archie said.

"I'm going to work today. Just leave me the fuck alone."

"Fuck you, then," he said as he walked out the door.

A robust man who never spent a day sick in his life, Archie saw sickness as weakness and an excuse to avoid work. He didn't understand headaches, and he knew Melissa didn't like her boss. But there were no other attorneys she could work for in Delbert, and a secretary's pay wouldn't make it worth the drive to Success.

Instead of going to work, Archie went to Campbell's Café and spent that morning drinking coffee and flirting with the waitress named Jenny. The missed day of work cost him the perfect attendance award he had received at the company Christmas dinner for the last five years, but watching Jenny's hips move beneath the snug fitting cotton of her dress set off an ache in Archie that embarrassed him. He couldn't get up from the table for fear of being noticed, and his erection refused to go away. The tightness of his jeans could only be relieved by one thing. Just before noon he slipped out of his booth and made it to the door. He called the White Law Firm from the payphone out on the square. Melissa could meet him at home, and he would apologize. They could make love for the rest of the afternoon. Things would be all right. They would find a way to pay their bills. But Randy Johnson answered Archie's call and told him Melissa wasn't at work and hadn't called in that morning.

Brought back from his memories, Archie sipped his coffee and waited on his breakfast. As Jenny scooted around the café, he noticed all the little things that had always seemed so neat about her. Her hair was never mussed, and she didn't wear all the make-up the other waitresses at Campbell's wore. She never came to work with hickies on her neck. Archie knew her twins had never met their father; the man had died before Jenny even knew she was pregnant.

6

Just before last Thanksgiving, Archie saw Jenny at the Piggly Wiggly over at Success buying groceries with her daughters. Archie started to speak with her. He wanted to meet the little girls he'd heard so much about, but when he saw Jenny reach into her purse and pull out the USDA food coupons, he understood. He'd never bought groceries with food stamps, but he could only imagine how embarrassing it must have been for her. Wallace and Owens was the only grocery store in Delbert, and Maude Nelson worked there as the bookkeeper. Maude lived next door to Archie. She'd installed a privacy fence—six inches across the property line on Archie's side—to separate their properties. A short woman, Maude had to stand on a five-gallon bucket placed next to the fence so she could see Archie while she chatted. The only person in town who spread more rumors than Maude was Delilah Marrs, the beautician married to Reverend Mooney Marrs. Maude let everyone in the county know who had bounced a check, or used food stamps to buy groceries, or hadn't paid the bill she sent for their monthly tabs. Archie figured Jenny must come to Success to buy all her groceries, or Maude would have told him about her. While keeping his distance, Archie watched as Jenny and her twins bagged their groceries and left the store.

After Thanksgiving, Archie went to the Department of Human Services at Success. Every year the agency hung the names of the children receiving aid on a tree for people in the community to adopt for Christmas. He pulled the tags with the names of Jenny's girls off the tree and spent his Christmas bonus on whatever they listed. The life insurance money he'd collected from Melissa's death had paid his mortgage, eliminated the debt on their vehicles and left him a surplus. But Archie had no one left, and he refused to spend the money on himself. He didn't deserve it. Jenny never knew who bought the presents. He respected her for her ability to get along alone—a skill he hadn't mastered yet—and he never wanted her to discover what he'd done. To eat breakfast at the café was a part of his routine he knew he'd give up rather than face her if she ever discovered his generosity.

The Friday after Christmas that year he saw Jenny asking everyone at the café if they knew who had bought the presents for her girls. No one accepted credit for the mystery gifts, so Jenny just thanked and hugged all of her customers, thinking surely she would get the right one. She never knew when she hugged Archie that she had.

As Jenny placed Archie's plate on his table, she said, "Did you hear what that damned Mooney Marrs did?" Without waiting for a response from Archie, she said, "He requested prayer for me and my girls, because Donna and Dana put a hex on Mooney Marrs Jr. Said they had participated in Devil worship."

Archie laughed. Reverend Mooney Marrs preached at the Delbert Nondenominational Free Worship Tabernacle. The church sat next door to his wife's beauty parlor. The sign in front of *God's House of Beauty* promised *A touch from above with every snip.* Delilah and the Reverend knew all the gossip in the town, and if the news got really bad, the good Reverend, with the best of intentions, asked for special prayer for Brother or Sister So-and-So, "Who as we all know is going through a special trial from the Devil himself."

Having your name included in a special prayer request or added to the prayer list on Sunday morning was Delbert's version of being selected the Mardi Gras King. Larry Cole held the record for the most requests due to his activities on behalf of the Democratic Party. He had five. Archie had two—both garnered within the month after Melissa's death—and that left him tied with the sheriff who was listed twice the month his daughter died from an accidental discharge of his firearm.

"I guess them girls hold the record now for being the youngest," Archie said.

"I'm taking that book away from them. I should have known better," Jenny said.

Archie picked up his fork and watched her as she walked away from his table. He hadn't been with another woman since Melissa's death. He had never cheated on Melissa, though he needed the past five years to convince himself of this truth. He never understood if he felt worse for leaving Jenny his last five dollars that morning after arguing with Melissa about their finances, or because Jenny had stirred feelings in him his wife couldn't. The marriage counselor had told them Archie's impotence was a psychological problem that would resolve itself. Their marital problems had created stress that interfered with his normal functions. But Archie had never expected a waitress at the local café to solve his problem.

***

Archie hung up the phone and rushed home that day in 1985. He knew now that Melissa needed to see some kind of doctor to help her with the headaches. Maybe a psychiatrist could help her, too. His impotency had been all in his head; the bulge in his Levis proved the counselor was right.

He walked in the door of the house.

"Melissa," he said as he walked in. She wasn't on the couch. He figured she'd be sitting there watching one of those daytime shows that always made fun of southern people.

He walked back to the bedroom.

"I think we need to get you an appointment with a doctor and have you examined," he said as he walked into the bedroom he shared with his wife. The odor of the room nauseated him.

Melissa lay tangled in the sheets. Her head tilted to her left, and her brilliant blue eyes, now a dull gray, stared unblinking at Archie as he stood in the door. He knew before he touched her that her skin would be cold.

Archie eased up to the bed, watching her eyes, hoping they would follow his movements around the room, praying they would blink, looking for some sign of life. The last words he'd said that morning before he left were "Fuck you." He backed away from the bed until he hit the wall. His knees buckled, letting his body slide down the knotty pine, until he sat on the floor.

One side of her face was swollen and looked like she'd had her wisdom teeth pulled. Archie saw a dark colored stain on the sheets where her hips lay flat on the bed. The smell. Archie had heard that sometimes, when people died, their bowels released, but he had never been the first to discover a body.

"I didn't mean what I said," he cried out loud. "I had good intentions. I just wanted you to get better."

The clock on the nightstand showed the time was 12:35. Eddie Leach would be writing people up at the factory for being late from

9

lunch. He sat on the floor and thought about what to do next. He knew he had to call someone. He needed to call work and tell them he wouldn't be back for a few days. But work no longer mattered.

On the tiled floor of the bedroom he spilled the breakfast Jenny had served him that morning. When he regained control of his stomach, Archie decided he should call the sheriff. He stood up and walked to the other side of the bed where he sat down again. His hand touched Melissa's stiff leg, and he jerked away, falling off the bed. The smell caused him to retch again. When he had nothing left in him, he got up and walked into the kitchen where he found an old green bucket they used to wash their cars. After removing the spatters from his own clothing, he filled the bucket with water and Mr. Clean and returned to the room.

As he scrubbed the floor, he decided to call Wilson Underwood. The sheriff of Jester County for over twenty years, Wilson would likely be out in the county and would take some time to get there. Archie looked at the dark stain on the sheets. He sat on the bed and kissed Melissa's forehead, then eased the sheets from around her arms and off the bed. He piled them in a heap at the door and took the green bucket back to the kitchen. After emptying the bucket in the back yard, Archie filled it again and returned to the bedroom. He couldn't let them see her like this.

He pulled the fitted sheet free from the corners of the bed, and stopped. Archie knew he needed to clean Melissa first. So he shifted her body. Her skin felt cold to his touch, and he had to straighten her arms and her leg so she didn't look so peculiar. After he closed her eyes, he eased her panties down off her torso; the odor caused him to retch again, but this time he had nothing left in his body to give.

Archie got back up and threw the panties into the pile at the foot of the bed. Then he spread her legs and used the washcloth to clean her. The dark brown liquid her body had expelled at her death had partially dried, and Archie gently scrubbed her thighs, and the hair around her vaginal area. He then turned her over and cleaned her from behind. He talked to her as he gently cleaned her cold skin. Rinsing the cloth repeatedly in the bucket caused the water to turn brown, so he emptied the bucket and returned to her side where he took his time and cleaned his wife. He knew he could never apologize for all that had happened that morning, but he hoped this would somehow show her that he was sorry.

While he sat on the side of the bed running the washcloth over her one last time, he decided to call the sheriff. Archie finally took the fitted sheet off the bed and lay Melissa off to the side of the wet spot on the mattress. He gathered the soiled linens and carried them outside. When he came back in, he went through her clothes and found her a clean pair of panties and a different nightgown. After he dressed her, Archie placed the call.

An hour later Sheriff Wilson Underwood stood next to Archie and watched as Pete Carter, the coroner, completed his investigation of the scene. Pete stooped over the body and opened one of Melissa's eyelids. He made a note on a form held in place on a clipboard.

"Does she have any prescription medicines? I need to collect them if she does," the coroner said.

"No. She wouldn't go to a doctor," Archie said.

The coroner motioned he needed some help, so Archie took Melissa by the ankles and helped Pete and the sheriff load Melissa's body onto the gurney. Her legs had stiffened, but her arms flailed awkwardly as they lifted her from the bed.

"Archie, I'm not gonna order an autopsy," Underwood said. "I'm closing this case. Go ahead and make the funeral arrangements."

"Does he know what happened?" Archie nodded towards the coroner.

"Pete says it was an aneurysm," Underwood said. "But the only way to know is with an autopsy. I can order one if you want, but they'll cut her to pieces."

"No. If I have a choice, don't. I wonder what you gotta do to become coroner?" Archie asked.

"Pete just filed and ran for the office. The state sent him to school after he won the election. I'll see you at the funeral, Archie." Underwood got in his truck and left.

After selecting a casket and deciding to bury Melissa in a plot at the Lamm's Chapel Cemetery, Archie returned to his empty house. The home sat in the middle of a small subdivision. Averaging between one thousand to twelve hundred square feet, the small houses all sat on concrete slabs, and their outside walls supported Masonite siding covered with cheap exterior paint that peeled every few years and left many of the homes looking like they needed a haircut rather than a paint job. The single-pane aluminum windows were no better than an empty hole in the wall. Barely bigger than the houses that sat on them, the lots could be mowed in five minutes with a push mower. Anyone who mowed the thin strip of grass that separated the cracker-box houses risked incurring the wrath of his fellow homeowner for blowing grass trimmings on the neighbor's carport.

As he pulled into his gravel driveway after making the funeral arrangements, he saw a group of people standing behind the privacy fence at Maude Nelson's. Archie had noticed the people standing outside as the ambulance left with Melissa's body. He'd even heard someone ask, "Why isn't he handcuffed?"

The small home he had shared with his wife seemed large and empty when he walked in the door. Archie could hear Maude Nelson outside, chatting with the neighbors and laughing. Laughing. How could anyone be laughing? His rage swelled and he burst through the closed door of the bedroom where he grabbed the linens and clothes and took them outside and piled them in the middle of his backyard. He carried the mattress out the back door and threw it on the heap. The chatter from behind the privacy fence stopped, and Archie saw Maude standing on her five-gallon bucket, surrounded by other pairs of eyes that peered over the top of the fence and watched him as he walked to the metal shed where he stored his push-mower. He grabbed his ax. From behind the fence someone gasped. With the ax in one hand and the gas can in the other, he turned back to the house. He could see through the thin cracks of the privacy fence as Maude fell off her bucket and the people with her scattered and ran. He laughed aloud. Then he took his ax inside and splintered the headboard in his bedroom. Every time he struck the wood, the ax buried up to the hilt. He kicked and struck and hammered and slung the splintered pieces through the closed window, shattering the glass and bending the aluminum windowpane. He would never spend a night with another woman on the bed he shared with Melissa.

After destroying the bed and hauling it out to his backyard, Archie soaked the wood and linens until he emptied the full can of gas, and then he tossed a lit match on top of the pile. The whoosh of the fire startled Archie, and he stood and watched as the angry flames and black smoke reached for the sky.

No one called the fire department.

Archie's rage set the rumor mill on fire in the town of Delbert. The sheriff and the coroner may have ruled Melissa's death a natural one, but the town formed its own opinion. Many said the sheriff was a fool for not ordering the autopsy, and Underwood's decision became an issue in the next election. Others said Archie had cleaned and burned the bed as soon as he could to destroy any evidence. Still, others claimed even if he hadn't killed her, he should have stayed home with her that day. Somehow, someway, the court of public opinion of Delbert always found Archie culpable for Melissa's death.

And the court always convened at Campbell's Café, where Archie couldn't bring himself to ask out a waitress who heard every day how he had killed his wife.

The prediction of an earthquake along the New Madrid Fault had set the city teeming with new life and new rumors to feed the mill. The city planned a festival for Friday, May 3rd, in order to call the attention of the populace to the need for preparation months in advance of the catastrophe. The festival would also promote the downtown district.

Jenny came back around and filled Archie's cup of coffee.

"I would like to take you and the girls to the Earthquake Festival," Archie said.

He could see her eyes moving over the lines of his face, and he wondered what she thought as she stood and looked at him. Was she wondering whether to believe the rumors? Did she even want a date? Archie had never seen her with a guy before, but he didn't think she was a lesbian; after all, she had two daughters. Was she worried she would wind up with another prayer request on Sunday morning?

"Mr. Campbell has two rules...no substitutions, and we are not supposed to date the customers. Well, three. We have to smoke out back. But he says if we break one rule, we might as well break them all." She stepped across the aisle and poured some more coffee, then turned and began to walk toward the back of the café where an elderly couple stood waiting to be checked out. Then she stopped, turned, and looked at Archie. "I guess you can have your fries today, and when does that festival start?"

Alligator Stew

The ringing phone brought Freddie straight up out of bed. He recognized Lee's voice on the other end.

"You been half-way right by me, you asshole, so say good-bye to your daughter before I blow her head off."

"Lee, send her on home and forget this shit." But Lee was already off the line and Charlotte came on. The tenor of her voice when she said, "Daddy," brought Freddie to his feet. She was scared. Mattie sat up from where she lay next to Freddie and turned on the overhead light.

"Charlotte—"

"Help me, Daddy." She was crying.

"Listen, Charlotte. Have you got your pistol?"

"Yes, Daddy. I do," she said between sobs.

"You kill that black bastard tonight."

"I don't know if I can."

"He's a dead man. I won't let him live another day. But you can't let him take you with him. Put a bullet between his eyes. Do you hear me?"

"I will, Daddy—"

"That's enough, old man. I got some business to take care of."

"I'm comin' to find you, Lee. Right now."

"Don't bother. I know I gotta kill you, too. I'll be right out, soon as I'm done with her. I'll stick you in the same hole, if I can find you."

"I'll be right here—"

The phone went dead. Freddie eased the receiver back to its place, while Mattie stood in front of him, wringing her hands. "Lee says he's gonna kill her, but he wanted her to say good-bye first. She says she has her pistol with her. They never said where they were."

"You can call Wilson. He can go out there," Mattie said.

"Go out where? If Lee kills her, he'll do it somewhere besides his house, and he said he was coming straight out here to get me

15

next." Freddie got up and pulled on his clothes. Out of the bureau drawer he pulled a Ruger Redhawk .357 and a snub-nosed Dan Wesson .38. The Ruger was in a shoulder holster he put on, and the Dan Wesson he stuffed in his hip pocket. Mattie had gone into the kitchen to start a pot of coffee.

"Hey, Mattie, has Charlotte got any clothes here?"

"Her closet is full of stuff from last time she was out. I washed and pressed them all."

"Bag'em up and throw 'em in the truck with my stuff."

"What?"

"If she kills that boy, we'll have to leave for a while. I can take her with me."

***

Earlier that day, Freddie had sat out in his tractor shed and watched as Sheriff Wilson Underwood pulled in. Wilson got out of the truck and looked around. After a few moments, Freddie whistled. The sheriff turned and walked across the yard to join him.

It wasn't that Freddie disliked people; he just didn't like being around them. People seemed to have far too much capacity for cruelty, so he preferred the wilderness. But there wasn't much of it left. All of the new contraptions—four-wheelers and airboats—made it impossible to get back far enough where no one could find you. But Wilson Underwood was one of the few people Freddie would tolerate.

After he entered the shed, Wilson went straight to the refrigerator. Freddie had taken an old Kenmore and ran a tap out the door. He stored a keg of Budweiser inside and kept frosted, quart mason jars in the freezer on top. A bottle of CO_2 sat next to the refrigerator, and a line from the cylinder snaked through the side of the Kenmore. Another refrigerator sat next to the tapped one. It held a replacement keg so Freddie would never be without cold beer. Wilson pulled a frosted jar from the freezer and looked at Freddie; he already held a full mug in his hands, so Wilson took the jar and poured one for himself. Freddie had supported Wilson since his first day in office, and Wilson showed his appreciation by helping himself to the beer without being asked, even when he was on duty.

16

"Freddie, what's this shit about you turning alligators loose over in the bottoms?"

Freddie laughed. He'd released those alligators three years ago, and Wilson was just now asking about them.

"Oh, those idiots down at the Co-op. I said somethin' about bringin' back some gator meat for the crawfish boil next spring, and it's been told around till it's come to this."

"You know it's illegal to import wildlife from another state and release it in Arkansas."

"Alligator stew, Wilson. I was plannin' on eatin' the damned things."

"I wish they'd release some gators in those bottoms. Help take care of the beavers so I wouldn't have to mess with paying the bounty on the damned things. I used to just throw them in the dumpster after paying the trappers their bounty. Then Bobbie Joe Willie started picking them up. I think he has a BBQ once a week now, over at Red Onion." Wilson laughed out loud. "I wonder if he gives them a fortune cookie that says 'That wasn't pork you were eating,' when they finish."

Freddie walked to the keg and drew a draft. He returned to his chair and offered Wilson a seat. Both men sat down.

"Beaver's good, and Bobbie Joe sure knows how to cook it. And they's some gators back in them bottoms. But I didn't put 'em there, and I don't want anyone to find out about 'em. Ever redneck in the damned county will be out there tryin' to shoot 'em."

"They killed one over at Coldstream a couple weeks back, but I guess you heard about that."

"That idiot game warden shouldn't have give them boys a ticket for that. You can't seine a catfish pond with an eight-foot alligator swimming around behind you."

"Wasn't my call, Freddie, but they could have had it trapped and removed," Wilson said. He took a drink of beer. Foam covered his lips. "How is Charlotte?"

"Her momma wants to ring her neck. That crazy-assed boyfriend of hers is about to run us silly."

"Lee just kinda took over where Sonny Howell left off. I know he's got a couple of meth labs over on Crowley's Ridge. I just ain't been able to locate them."

"If I hear Charlotte say anything, I'll give ya a call. She winds up out here about ever other weekend, runnin' from that black bastard. He's big as an ox, but all he can do is beat on a woman. He don't dare come out here after her. Or with her."

Wilson turned up his beer and left nothing but a bit of foam in the bottom. Freddie stood and reached for the sheriff's jar, but Wilson shook his head. Freddie knew the routine. Wilson always drank one, but no more.

"I been worried about her, and about you."

"You ain't gotta worry about me. Charlotte doesn't act like she's on that shit. At least she hasn't lost any weight that I can tell."

"I don't mean like that. I don't want that boy disappearing before I can bust him."

"I'm not like Pawpaw, Wilson. If Lee treated Charlotte right, I wouldn't mind the color of his skin. He hurts her, and I'll peel him right out of it. Won't care what color he is. I don't want any more family secrets buried in those bottoms, but you know I won't hesitate to add another if he hurts her."

"I worry more about her being there when I bust him."

"He's gotten away with layin' hands on my daughter a few times too many, Wilson. Sides, she swears she never goes around where he cooks the shit."

"She tell you that?"

"She's my son, too, you know. I never got to raise a boy, so we're close like that. She cried on my shoulder the day after she lost her cherry. She sure didn't talk to her momma about it. I don't cast judgment or try to tell her what to do, but she won't lie to me, either. And if I don't wanna know the truth, I don't ask."

"I know that. Have you heard from Charlotte today?"

"You been makin' small talk when somethin's wrong?" Freddie leaned forward, paying a bit more attention to the sheriff's words.

"Heard Lee is pretty strung out. Someone said they had a big fight out at Scatter Creek last night, and they had to pull him off her.

She cut him good—took fifty stitches. I'm not here to see her. I'm here to tell you if she shows up, he'll likely be right behind her."

"Let him come on out, Wilson. He's welcome here." Freddie went to the keg again. "The boy won't cause me any problems. He knows the keg sits right here in the shed, just like it always has."

Wilson got up to go. "I doubt he'll be coming to drink beer, Freddie. Beaver Howell hates me now after what happened with Sonny. I don't wanna lose our friendship, but I'll do my job if anything happens."

"What about my daughter? They's been plenty happenin' to her. Why don't you do your fuckin' job and do somethin' about that before she ends up like Nancy Davis, instead of comin' out here and mouthin' you'll bust Charlotte, too? You afraid someone's gonna call you a bigot cause you arrested the only nigger in Jester County?"

"Don't talk that way, Freddie. Charlotte won't press charges, and I can't do anything till she does. Besides, I think she's been trying to get Lee to quit. Akens, the county parole officer, dropped by the Narcotics Anonymous meeting the other day to see how many of his parolees were there and saw Lee and Charlotte, both."

"I know there's a few family secrets buried out in those bottoms, Wilson, and I know your granddad was a part of it. My Pawpaw may have been a bigot. But that doesn't make me one, any more than it makes you one. Lee won't come out here causin' me problems, and if he does, you can do your job, but it won't help that bastard one bit."

Wilson extended his hand. Freddie shook it.

"Stick around. Drink some beer with me," Freddie said.

"I gotta get back to town and get to work on this earthquake preparedness grant. I don't believe anyone can predict an earthquake, but, living on a fault line, it sure won't hurt to be ready. You going to Louisiana soon? Don't you go once your crops are in?"

"First thing in the mornin'," Freddie said as they walked to the sheriff's truck. "I'm gettin' away a bit early this year. You'll have to come out and eat with us when I get back. I'll have a big mess of crappie. They call them perch down there, or sacalait." Once he had his crops laid by, Freddie spent the rest of the summer back in the swamp, brushing out his duck blinds and running trotlines and nets,

19

coming out occasionally to check on his wife and crops. During late spring he made an annual pilgrimage to spend a couple weeks on a houseboat in the Atchafalaya Basin in Louisiana, running crawfish traps and catching snakes for laboratories.

"I always heard you slip some snake in the frying pan," Wilson said.

"I'll see to it you get fish. I promise." Both men chuckled.

"Call me if you need me, Freddie."

As Wilson drove off, Freddie walked back to the shed and filled his mug one more time.

***

After he grabbed the pistols, Freddie walked outside. For the rest of the night, minutes would seem like hours. He wondered how long to wait before going to find Charlotte.

Life would be different after tonight. Even if Charlotte survived and didn't kill Lee, it was a matter of time before this happened again, only next time Lee might go too far. If Freddie could find him, Lee wouldn't live to see the sun rise, whether he killed Charlotte or not.

His biggest regret was the sheriff; after tonight Freddie could never trust Wilson again. They'd been lifelong friends, like brothers. But Freddie knew Wilson would do his job, no matter who he had to arrest.

Freddie watched the shimmering glow from the lights of Delbert. He could see any vehicles approaching miles away down the straight dirt road that led to their simple home, but sitting and waiting would drive him nuts, so he went to the tractor shed and fired up the Farmall. After he gassed it up, he pulled it around front. He didn't know what he'd need it for, but he wanted it ready.

Freddie walked back to the shed and pulled a box of bullets out of a cabinet. They were .38 shells that he could shoot from either pistol. The Ruger was loaded with .357 rounds. If he needed more, he'd have to shoot the lighter loads. But he knew he was more accurate with those, and he didn't need the magnum to kill this snake. He could smell the breakfast Mattie cooked back in the house.

Whenever a problem arose, Mattie went to the kitchen and cooked or cleaned. It kept her busy and her mind occupied. Freddie wished he could do the same. He could think of nothing else to do, and he couldn't go to the kitchen. Mattie would want to talk. So he went to the keg, poured a beer and sat down.

She was a good woman, and he felt bad about Louisiana. Not all of the family secrets were buried in the Hatchie Coon Bottoms.

***

After the sheriff had left that morning, Freddie drove his old "H" Farmall back into the swamp. The river was down—had been down for some time—and the bogs were dry, so he drove right up to the edge of the Blue Hole. Freddie had never been to Vietnam, but he claimed to have flashbacks, and he winked every time he told that lie. Anytime a helicopter or crop duster flew over, he'd jump behind a log or run and dive into a slough and holler, "Incoming." His scoliosis kept him from being drafted, so he'd settled for taking over the family farm and the Schugtown Co-op out at Lester—a wide spot in the road in Jester County, just south of Delbert, Arkansas.

He got off the tractor and walked over to a large brush pile where he pulled out an old pirogue he'd brought back from Louisiana many years ago. After dragging the wooden canoe to the edge of the lake, he went back to get the paddle he'd left in the pile. Sitting in the middle of the pirogue, he eased out into the water.

The Blue Hole used to be part of the main channel of the St. Francis River. The bottom dropped precipitously five feet out from the bank on the north end where Freddie kept his canoe. He'd used a depth-finder once while fishing with Wilson in the sheriff's new bass boat. The water dropped off to nearly fifty feet, and Freddie loved to swim in the depths that remained cool even in the hottest part of summer. Between the knees and trunks of the cypress trees lay the skeletons of giant sweet gum and water oaks that had rotted or were felled by high winds—the hollow logs half-submerged in the water. Few people ever made it back to the Blue Hole. You had to know where it was to get to it, and for most of the year, you had to pull your boat through a mile of swamp.

21

Now the lake was isolated from the river until the floodwaters came again in winter, or until a rare summer flood happened, or until water was released at the Wappapello Dam in Missouri.

Freddie wished the bottoms were wider. He knew the St. Francis Delta was rich and fertile enough to support more game, but the bottoms weren't wide enough to provide a wilderness sanctuary like the Atchafalaya.

A large cottonmouth sunned on an old sweet gum that jutted from the bank out into the deep water. The log the snake rested on was hollow all the way through, and Freddie had hogged more than one big flathead out of the empty shell. But the last time he'd gone to check, Gertie was up in it. Gertie was a gift from Thibodeaux, a six-foot female gator that nearly broke his leg when he tried to release her. She liked to swim up in the log and hide. Freddie had released a bull, too, a smaller one that had grown and moved out of the bottoms, and he was sure the gator killed at Coldstream was his.

The sheriff was a bit slow on the uptake, either that or word was slow to get around. But Freddie was confident Wilson had known about the gators all along and just used it as an excuse to come talk about Charlotte.

Gertie hatched a couple of broods, though, and Freddie was confident another male swam the river somewhere. Maybe a larger male had moved in and forced the other bull out, but something had mated with Gertie. Freddie wasn't gonna take any chances, though, and made plans to haul back another pair when it cooled off again in the fall. The heat made it impossible to haul them on a long trip in the summer.

The pirogue floated up alongside the log, and Freddie eased up to the front. He allowed the canoe's slow, forward motion to carry him within reach of the cottonmouth. His hand flashed and he had the snake behind its huge head. It writhed and whipped about and released a dank, musky odor as it bared its fangs and revealed the snow-white lining of its jaws. Freddie had caught hundreds of snakes, and he'd paid a painful price many times while hogging catfish when he'd stick his hand up a flooded, hollow log feeling for a flathead, just to be bitten by a cottonmouth. He didn't want to kill the snake—the laboratory at LSU would pay a bundle for a cottonmouth that big. But he didn't have a burlap bag to haul it off. If he didn't kill it, the snake would end up back on the log again, and Freddie didn't want to compete with a cottonmouth that big the next time he went fishing.

Only about four feet long, the moccasin was thick in its body all the way down to its blunt tail. As he held on to the snake, he reached with his other hand and pulled out his knife. He stuck the blade up in behind the two-inch fangs, and the snake bit down, shooting two streams of mucous-green venom over the side of the boat and out into the water. The poison floated on the surface like a grease spill. If that snake had hit him, he'd have never made it back to the tractor. After catching a poisonous snake, Freddie always milked it, that way if he made a mistake and got bit, the snake wouldn't have much venom left.

Freddie had caught snakes all his life, and he'd only recently discovered he could make money doing it. Catching snakes had been his way of being accepted when little.

His mother always scolded him for being too active. "You'll hurt your back," she'd say. She knew the curve of his spine wasn't right.

The kids in his class picked on him, and although his older brother, Teddie Mac, ran interference, Teddie couldn't always be there. All of the kids in school were scared of snakes, though, and the first time he caught a copperhead at the schoolhouse, he'd chased them all over the yard. After that, they left him alone and would even take him with them as they prowled the playground looking for reptiles to scare the teachers with.

Holding the head of the snake at a safe distance so a fang couldn't snag him, he eased deeper into the Blue Hole. He knew he was close, so he clicked in his throat, making the sound of a baby gator. The alligator grunted. Then he saw the large mound of dirt and leaves. His eyes had to search and focus before he finally saw her, perched on top of a nest where she sunned. He stood up and tossed the cottonmouth by its tail. It landed a foot in front of Gertie. The alligator lunged for the snake, snapping its body in two as the snake buried its venom less fangs in the leathery skin of the alligator's jaws.

Easing the pirogue back out to the deep end of the lake, Freddie stripped, then jumped out of the boat. The tea-colored surface felt warm till about ten feet down, where he hit the cooler water that missed the direct light of the sun. Wilson called this the *thermocline*. The cold water eased the constant ache in Freddie's back as his strong arms pulled him down into the cooler depths. Able to stay underwater longer than anyone he knew, Freddie dove deep until he touched the bottom. He opened his eyes. The water was not muddy, but not clear—black, like water in a stump. They had named the Blue Hole after his grandpa's bluetick hounds that always treed back along its banks, not for the color of its waters. And Pawpaw's hounds didn't always tree raccoons.

Pawpaw had been an Imperial Wizard with the Klan. Some of the hunts they'd had in the bottoms weren't always for wild game. But the local Klan had died with his Pawpaw, and those who refused to accept the changing times had joined the Posse Comitatus and moved over into the hills around Smithville, and even further west to Harrison. Some had even abandoned Arkansas for Idaho after the siege that happened at Flippin, Arkansas, during the early eighties.

The farmers out at the Co-op ribbed Freddie constantly about Charlotte dating the only black man in Jester County. They all assumed Freddie would be like Pawpaw. But none of them knew about Joue.

Freddie burst up through the surface and looked around for the pirogue. The small wooden vessel was nearly impossible to climb in without tipping, but he'd learned the trick from Thibodeaux. He eased back into the boat where he made a pillow of his clothes and stretched out naked in the sun to sleep and dry off.

He tried to imagine how these woods looked back when his grandfather first moved into the area and ran steamboats up the old channel from the Mississippi. Back then the river was lined with miles and miles of cypress trees so old and huge that five men in a circle holding hands couldn't have reached around them. His Pawpaw had never been to California and seen a redwood or a sequoia, but the old man claimed the trees in those bottoms were just as big.

Freddie had seen pictures of redwoods, and knew that as big as the cypress trees may have been, they couldn't have compared. But he never told his grandfather the truth. Pawpaw had been wrong about a lot of things, but he believed in the grandeur of the Old South. He'd seen the plantations, the old steam riverboats, the lynching and cross burnings. He'd met those who claimed to have fought in the war of northern aggression. When just a nubbin, Pawpaw had traveled with his own grandfather to the reunions in Forrest City of those who proudly claimed to have ridden—during and after the war—with Nathan Bedford Forrest, a man many blamed for creating the Klan. He'd lived through the riots and wars of desegregation. He'd cheered Wallace's stand at the University of Alabama doors and cursed Eisenhower when he sent the National Guard to integrate Central High School in Little Rock. He died believing Arkansas would someday secede again; he died believing every black man was a "blue-gum nigger" and deserved to be lynched for even looking at a white woman.

His Pawpaw would have disowned him over the mulatto child Freddie had fathered and went to see every summer, over the Creole woman named Ellie Jean who welcomed him home any time he could slip away to Louisiana, over the voodoo witchcraft Ellie Jean practiced that Pawpaw would have called devil worship. But deep in the Atchafalaya, nearly everyone practiced some form of voodoo. Pawpaw would have been ashamed to know that a black man now lived in Jester County, and his great granddaughter dated him. Freddie loved his Pawpaw like no one he had ever known, but he knew progress could only happen with the death of the old ways, and the people who kept the old ways alive.

He had tried to talk Charlotte out of dating Lee, but his reasons had nothing to do with the color of the man's skin. He knew Lee didn't have a job. When people don't work, but always have money, they have to make it someway. Charlotte called her father a bigot and told him to mind his own business, so he shut up. But she kept coming out to the farm, more and more often, it seemed. Lee wouldn't chase her there, and Freddie knew it wasn't because the man was scared of him. Lee would only mess with someone he could bully, and there is a difference in fear and avoiding a fight.

After the third weekend of Charlotte coming home in the middle of the night, Freddie bought her a pistol, a small snub-nosed .38. He'd thought about an automatic .25, but those jammed too often, and he wanted her to get off six shots if she needed too. At first, she

25

just laughed at her father, and then she picked up the pistol and spun the cylinder.

"You got some shells?"

"Let's run down to the bridge. You won't be able to hit anything more than ten feet away, but we can break it in," Freddie said. He pulled a box of cartridges out of his hip pocket.

"Did you ice some beer down, Daddy?"

"I run some out of the keg into some plastic milk jugs."

She laughed. "I got some Budweiser on ice in my cooler. I'll throw it in the truck." She got up and walked out the door.

Freddie wanted his son in Louisiana to meet his daughter. Freddie believed in the bond of family and that brothers and sisters stood together. Charlotte never had a brother – her mother could only have the one child. Although Joue only saw his father a few weeks each year, he knew Freddie and loved him. A big, powerful young man, Joue had just turned seventeen, three years younger than Charlotte. If Joue were here now, Freddie knew he could send Joue out to catch Lee. And he would. Although Joue was half-Creole, the Cajuns had taken him in as one of their own and raised his son by the old ways. Back in the Atchafalaya, the difference between Cajun and Creole was a matter of pedigree that didn't matter to anyone. Ellie Jean's spells were respected, even feared. Being in her favor was always good, and the boy was easy to like. He was good with a knife and could skin a man's eyelids before he could blink.

Jean Thibodeaux gave Joue a job working with the crawfish farm, and he'd worked hard as any man since he'd turned thirteen. Joue lived in the bottoms near Labadieville and traveled to Eunice to work crawfish during the season. Thibodeaux gave him a crop bonus when the season was over, so Joue made good money. He'd been accepted early into Nicholls State University where he wanted to study aquaculture and the folk history of Mardis Gras. Attending Nicholls State would allow Joue to stay close to his mother, a beautiful Creole woman who survived on a widow's military pension—she'd lost her husband in Vietnam. Freddie tried to talk Joue into coming to Arkansas and attending Arkansas State at Jonesboro. He told Joue he could come stay with him, work on the farm while attending classes.

Joue knew the problems that would cause.

"When your wife finds out about me, that you have a black son in Louisiana come home to live under her roof, that you still see my momma when you come down in the summer, she'll kick both of us out."

"She don't have to know I see your momma when I come down. And Mattie would be upset, but I believe she would accept you. She suspects I have someone down south anyways, but she doesn't believe in divorce. She always wanted Charlotte to have a brother, but we couldn't have any more kids. We'd find a way to make it work, son," Freddie said.

"But what about your daughter? How will she feel when she learns you cheated on her mother, with a Creole?"

Freddie didn't tell Joue that Charlotte dated a black man; that the color of Joue's skin wouldn't matter to Charlotte. Charlotte had always accepted her father with all his flaws. All that would matter to her was the infidelity, and she would forgive Freddie, eventually. But to bring Joue home with him to live would rip his family apart, and Freddie knew Joue was right. Freddie's guilt for cheating on Mattie and for not acknowledging Joue grew every day, and each year he found himself anticipating the time with his son even more than the time he spent with Ellie Jean. He didn't want to hurt Mattie, but he wouldn't give up Ellie Jean or Joue. For now, an education in Louisiana would have to do for his son, but he still wanted his two children to meet before he died and Charlotte discovered her inheritance would be split with a half-brother from Louisiana.

As he dozed in the sun, Freddie thought of his trip south. It would be nice to get away from all the bullshit at the co-op and see Ellie Jean again. He planned to leave early in the morning and was already packed. Freddie forgot about his meeting with the sheriff as the pirogue drifted lazily over to the south bank, nudged along by the hot summer breeze. In the distance he heard a crop duster, and he whispered, "Incoming," as he slid over the side of the pirogue and back into the water.

***

Through the open doors of the shed Freddie saw lights coming up the road. He slipped out and shot the yard light so no one could see. Mattie yipped from inside the house. Shimmying up an oak tree in the yard, Freddie crawled out to a spot where he'd have a clean shot at anyone pulling into the drive. He held the Ruger in his right hand.

Charlotte's car pulled in and she jumped out of the door. Freddie shouted her name as he dropped out of the tree, and Mattie ran out the door of the house.

"Where is he?" Freddie said as Charlotte ran to him. "Are you hurt?" She had been crying, but no more.

"He's in the trunk, Daddy."

"Dead?"

Charlotte nodded. "Right through the gap in those front teeth."

"Take her inside and change her clothes," he said to Mattie. "Better yet, strip right here so I can take your clothes with me."

"Daddy!"

"There could be some blood splatter on them, and you can't track that into the house. Shuck them off. Everything."

She stripped as Mattie ran to the clothesline for a sheet to wrap her in.

"Do you know where I keep the pirogue down at the Blue Hole?" Charlotte nodded at her daddy as she hid her breasts behind her right arm and her left hand covered the small patch between her legs. Her mother ran to her and wrapped her in a sheet as Freddie gathered her clothes and tossed them into the car. Mattie now held her daughter in a bear hug, kissing her cheeks and crying.

"Go in and eat some breakfast. Your mother's been cooking ever since Lee called. Give me about thirty minutes, then bring my truck down and get me."

Charlotte nodded her head.

"I'm already packed and loaded. We'll leave town after you pick me up."

"What we gonna do, Daddy?"

"We go to Louisiana, just like I planned. We got people there we can stay with for a few weeks. Family you've never met."

"They'll find Lee, Daddy. We gotta call Wilson."

"Leave that to me. Now go with your momma and do as I say."

Freddie jumped in the little Ford Taurus and backed out the driveway. The transmission had been slipping on the piece of shit. He could feel it slipping now as he sped away. With his luck, the transmission would quit before he could get into the bottoms. He took some odd twists and turns as he drove, and even though the river was low, the little compact couldn't navigate the usual roads he traveled. But he knew another way in.

He backed up to the Blue Hole and parked close to the water. A light came on when he opened the trunk. Lee's lifeless eyes were open, staring at the spare tire, his face frozen in a gap-toothed grin. The back of his head was a gelatinous goo. Freddie crushed the bulb of the trunk light. There was no moon, so he waited till his eyes adjusted to the dark, then walked around to the front of the car to disconnect and remove the battery. The battery would eventually poison the water, and he could use it back home on one of his old tractors. He removed his clothes and piled them on top of a cypress stump at the edge of the woods, and then he stripped the body in the trunk of the car. He tossed Charlotte's clothes on the bank near the water and threw Lee's bloody clothes on top. He made a small fire, adding dry twigs, branches and leaves.

Careful not to spill any blood on the ground, he eased Lee's body out of the trunk and into the water. Grasping the hair of the carcass, Freddie swam out and down the shore of the lake. He didn't want to use the pirogue for fear of leaving blood in it. His feet finally came to rest on the log where he'd caught the cottonmouth earlier, and he prayed Gertie was still laying eggs in her nest and not holed up in the tree, not yet. Finding the hole in the side of the log through which he'd hogged many big catfish, he pulled the body under water and stuffed it in the old hollow tree.

The log would hold the body until everything was gone. Gertie would take care of the rest. She would eat bones and all. The snapping turtles and channel cats would help, too. All were carrion eaters, and nothing would be left after a few weeks.

They would toss Charlotte's pistol off the Mississippi River Bridge in Baton Rouge.

Charlotte could claim self-defense if they called the sheriff, but no one would believe her. The whole community would think she lied to cover for her father. People had a way of making up their minds about what happened in Jester County, and facts only got in the way with what people wanted to believe. Freddie had felt no disgrace over Charlotte's black boyfriend. If anything, he was proud she felt confident enough to be open about her relationship with Lee. She had proven she was stronger than her father. He hoped it might make her more willing to accept Joue as her brother.

After swimming back to the car, he stirred the fire to make sure the clothes were completely gone. Not even a single thread was left. Then he washed the ashes off into the lake. With the car in neutral, he pushed it into the water, where it disappeared down the steep incline into the depths of the Blue Hole. That was the best place for a Ford, anyway. He left the windows down and trunk lid open, hoping the water might wash away any trace of DNA evidence and blood. He would return after he came back from Louisiana and swim down into the depths to close the trunk lid.

He saw lightning flash in the distance and heard a rumble of thunder. A good rain was just what he needed to erase any tire tracks. He put his clothes back on and sat on a cypress stump to wait.

Freddie's mouth watered as he thought of the crawfish and stuffed red snapper he'd eat when he and Charlotte made it to Louisiana. The trip would be different, but now they both had secrets buried deep in the swamps, and he knew it was time to be honest with his daughter. As he listened for the truck, he heard the sounds of the night around him: the clicks of baby alligators, the bass throbbing of a bullfrog, the slap of a beaver's tail on the water. He watched the willowy outline of a mink hopping along the edge of the water, its head held high, nostrils testing the wind for a hint of blood. And as he looked out at the depths of the Blue Hole that now hid another family secret, he wished the bottoms were bigger.

Goat and Dumplins

Clayton Lee came home from Delbert Elementary School on the second day of class in early August and surprised his father. "I want a goat," the boy said.

Jimmy Lee began his career as a math teacher at Delbert High school in 1980, and after ten years in the classroom, he couldn't think of anything that would surprise him. But he never anticipated Clayton's request for a goat.

"Why do you want a goat?" Jimmy asked his eight-year-old son.

"We studied earthquakes in class today. Last October there was an earthquake in San Francisco that hurt over three thousand people. Peru and Romania both had earthquakes in May. Then in June, Iran had an earthquake that killed fifty thousand people and destroyed every house for miles. In July, the Philippines had an earthquake that killed sixteen hundred people. There is something about the planets lining up this year that's causing these earthquakes, and we live in the middle of an earthquake zone, Daddy. Did you know that?"

"Yes, I've heard about all of this." Jimmy stifled his grin. Apparently his son had paid attention in class that day.

"My teacher said that when we have an earthquake, we won't be able to get any food. We need to store some bottled water and supplies, and if we have a goat, we can milk it and make cheese. We can even cook it if we have to."

"We can do the same thing with a cow, son," Jimmy said.

"But my teacher said a cow would eat too much. There might not be any grain or hay left, and a goat can eat anything."

"I'll see what I can do," Jimmy said.

"We need a goat right now, Daddy. That earthquake can happen anytime. Some scientist predicted the one in San Francisco, and the same guy says we'll have one right here in December. We have got to be ready. I'm gonna check our fences out in the pasture right now."

31

Jimmy chuckled at his son's exuberance. He admired the boy's enthusiasm. Children are insulated from the burden of rituals and routines, and every novelty adds a new excitement to their lives. During the past couple of years as his marriage had slowly seemed to implode, lethargy had taken over the relationship he shared with his wife. Although Jimmy had always been a faithful husband, he felt a new vigor when Mrs. Anderson, a science teacher at the high school where he worked, had told him her husband was leaving town for the weekend and invited him to stop by.

Gayle Anderson had asked Jimmy to come by her house Saturday while her husband attended a coaching seminar in Memphis. Jimmy didn't always cater to his son's wants, but he saw an opportunity to teach Clayton a valuable lesson about maturity and accepting responsibility for his actions—and an opportunity for an alibi to get away from the house Saturday morning. A goat was something Clayton couldn't just play with a few times, and then toss aside and forget like his other toys. Of course, neither was a married woman, especially one with a husband as big as Bull Anderson.

Any man who developed an infatuation for a married woman at his place of employment was a fool. Jimmy knew this. Gayle's husband was the principal, as well as the head basketball coach, and Bull Anderson was not only his boss, but big enough to stand under the goal and dunk a basketball without even jumping.

As beautiful as Bull was big, Gayle was petite, with implanted breasts, a brand new nose, and carrot-red hair. She wore dresses slit at the neck and thigh, and the slits came closer together every day. That tantalizing glimpse of white neckline and exposed thigh drove all the boys in the school mad, and Jimmy knew just how they felt.

Gayle had a problem, though. As beautiful as she was, no one would risk more than a glance her way as long as Bull was around. At first, Jimmy ignored her advances. But then came the weekend Bull was leaving for Memphis. Gayle had planned for this event for some time. She caught Jimmy alone in the teacher's lounge early that week, and explained, in vivid detail, what she wanted to do to him; all he had to do was show up at her home Saturday after Bull left.

Buying Clayton a goat would provide the perfect excuse for getting away from the house. But Jimmy didn't know if he could follow through or not. Cheating on Rachel, his wife and the mother of his son, would have severe consequences if he were caught.

Rachel would never have considered plastic surgery to improve her appearance. She never dressed up, never wore anything racy, and seldom wore perfume. Rachel had helped Jimmy stretch the fences that would now hold Clayton's goat. She had worked by Jimmy's side after they bought their land, and together they built their house and cleared the twenty acres behind it. After working all day on the property, she would cook supper, and then when the evening meal was done, she cleared the table and washed the dishes. She made sure Clayton did his homework. Rachel's heart broke the day that Clayton told her he was too big for her to kiss him goodnight. So after he bathed each night, she knelt by his bed and prayed with him.

However, Clayton was also their biggest problem. Rachel insisted that Jimmy should not punish the boy; she wanted Clayton to do the right thing because it was right, not for fear of punishment. This created a major rift with her husband, for Jimmy believed a spanking was far more effective than talking for half an hour to a child who didn't understand and couldn't reason through the logical process of decision making. The situation had strained their marriage, eliminated their sex life, and caused Jimmy to think of things he should not have been considering. He wanted to go to Gayle's when she called. He wanted to see if a woman could really do all the things she said. He wanted to show her what he could do for her.

Jimmy had never been to a livestock auction, and he had no idea where to buy a goat, so he called an old friend. Bobbie Joe Willie was another bear of a man who knew everything about anything that wasn't published in a book. Jimmy had only seen Bobbie Joe once when he didn't have a chew of tobacco in his mouth, and that day his jowls had hung so loosely along his jaw line that he reminded Jimmy of an English bulldog. Broken repeatedly by inebriated patrons of the Red Onion Tavern—a honky-tonk his family had owned since Arkansas was re-admitted to the Union—Bobbie Joe's wide, flat nose extended from one corner of his smile to the other, but did not extend past his chin.

An old river rat, Bobbie Joe Willie ran nets on the St. Francis River and had free fish fries once a week at his bar. The cookouts had been a tradition for over twenty years. The wives of his best customers all attended the midweek church services on Wednesday nights, making it easy for their husbands to slip out without having to make an excuse. The fish were salty enough to have been soaked in a brine, but that only sold more beer. Bobbie Joe had guided duck hunters, set trap lines and fished for years, proudly boasting that he'd never held a job for more than a week. He said owning a tavern wasn't a legitimate job. It was like having a hunting ground for women year round.

Bobbie Joe Willie would know where to find a goat and would understand Tommy's need for an alibi. So Jimmy called Bobbie Joe at his little shack behind the tavern. The phone rang three times before it was answered.

"This is Bobbie Joe. What do you want?"

"This is Jimmy Lee. I need to buy a goat for my boy."

"Old Claudie Walker has always got some goats for sale. He lives over on Big Island, only son of a bitch that's lived on the river longer than me."

"Reckon we could go over there Saturday morning and haul one of them back to the tavern? I'd have to pick it up later that day."

"Yup, I gotta catch pen out back where you can leave it. But we gotta make damned sure we get there early and leave shortly thereafter." Then Bobbie Joe Willie hung up the phone.

***

Gayle cornered Jimmy in the teacher's lounge that Friday as he tried to steal a jelly donut.

"Are you coming to my place Saturday?" She slid her hand up and grabbed the handle of Tommy's zipper.

"I'm supposed to go buy some livestock that morning with a friend. Just page me after Bull leaves," Jimmy said. Gayle pinned him next to the door and pressed up against him. Jimmy saw her bright red lips, the amber of her areolas as he looked down her dress, the pink discoloration of the scar from her implant surgery. She kissed him.

"Going to buy some cattle? Are you a cowboy?" She ran her arms around him and squeezed his ass. He bolted through the door and bumped into Bull Anderson.

"You got some raspberry jelly on your mouth," Bull said.

Jimmy wiped Gayle's lipstick off his lips as he slid away to the safety of his classroom.

When he got home that night, Jimmy's mind was on Gayle, until Rachel showed him what she'd bought at Victoria's Secret over in Success earlier in the day.

"You've been so distant lately. Have I done something wrong?" she asked.

"No, everything's screwed up at work."

"I thought I would do something special for you tonight. I even bought some of those videos you like to watch."

Rachel put Clayton to bed early for a Friday night, and they didn't quite make it through the first video before they called it an evening, too.

***

Jimmy left the house shortly before ten the next morning and went straight to Red Onion. If anyone ever saw Bobbie Joe Willie in a good mood, they'd wonder if he were sick.

"You're late," he said. "We gotta hurry so we can get there and be gone before eleven."

"We can buy a goat some other time if you've got something more important to do today."

Jimmy didn't think Gayle could top Rachel's performance from the night before. He could go home, turn off his pager, and spend the rest of the day with his wife and son. That was the right thing to do. But he kept hearing those words Gayle had whispered in his ear. He could smell her perfume, see her white skin. He remembered the way her breasts bounced as she strutted down the hall of the school, how her nipples stretched the fabric of her lace bras and silk blouses, and he just knew he would never be caught.

"It's not that," Bobbie Joe said. "We don't wanna be there for lunch. His wife is a nasty cook. Besides, I been humpin' her for a while now, and I feel uncomfortable spendin' too much time with a man when I been humpin' his wife."

"Oh. I can relate to that," Jimmy said.

They loaded up in Bobbie Joe's old Chevy truck with the white livestock rack and took off. Bobbie Joe didn't care if Jimmy left the goat with him for a while. But he warned that he'd have a goat roast if Jimmy waited too long to come and get it. "My customers at the Red Onion will eat anything that's free."

After they left the main highway, they drove down the levee, dodging deep, gouged out ruts in the road. Bobbie Joe dipped off the side so suddenly that Jimmy yelped.

"You trying to kill us?"

Bobbie Joe Willie laughed and spit out the window. They traveled down a turn road along the edge of a bean field, with a narrow ditch to their left, and the wood line that marked the edge of the river just ahead.

"Isn't it kinda dangerous screwing a married woman, then going to her house to buy a goat from her husband?" Jimmy asked.

"Damned right it is. I see that silly bastard every day at the Red Onion Tavern, and I don't let him outta my sight, either. You never know what a jealous husband is capable of. Seen too many of 'em at the tavern. But he drinks a lot of beer and he always pays his tab, so I let him in."

Jimmy knew if anyone told Bull what he was about to do, Bull would kill him. If Rachel found out, she would leave him. He couldn't decide which would be worse.

The truck entered the woods and drove on for three miles before they finally came to an old, wooden bridge across the Arkansas Ditch. The ditch ran on a convergent path with the St. Francis River until they finally met, like the vortex of a *V*. Claudie Walker lived at the junction of the river and the ditch, having squatted on the ground that he lived on—according to Bobbie Joe—since Noah got off the Ark.

After crossing the bridge, they turned back left and drove another fifteen minutes. Jimmy checked his pager to make sure it was on. Gayle would page him to let him know Bull had left for Memphis, and he was supposed to get there as quick as he could. He thought of

Gayle's pale thighs, thought of Rachel's tanned body in that leopard print camisole last night, thought of the vows he took on his wedding day; he thought of how hurt Rachel would be if she ever found out, thought of how hurt he'd be if Bull found out.

And he thought of how much trouble he could avoid if he'd just go home.

Claudie Walker lived in a shotgun style house. The color of the rusted tin roof nearly matched the ancient brick pattern of the brown tarpaper on the walls. To keep it above the hundred-year flood mark the house floated four feet above the ground on stilts. The front and back doors stood wide open, and if you walked up to the front door, you could see all the way through to the backyard.

Three Walker coonhounds slept up under the porch and thumped their tails as Bobbie Joe and Jimmy pulled into the yard. Twenty or so game roosters pulled at the end of tethers attached to their legs and anchored to fifty-five gallon drums in the front yard. With only inches separating them, the roosters strained to reach each other. Two goats sunned lazily on the front porch. As Bobbie Joe Willie parked his truck, a goat got up and walked into the house.

"Look at that," Bobbie Joe said. "He keeps the house open so the goats can walk through to the backyard. Says it burns the fat off 'em if they have to walk too far."

A small television antenna jutted out of an open window. On the metal arm that supported the antenna sat two chickens, resting in the sun with their eyes half closed. Partially buried off to one side of the tarpaper shack was an old van. Someone had shoveled dirt up along the sides and on the top of the van to bury it. The back end of the van, with both doors open, allowed easy access to the inside where two more goats nibbled at what was left of the vinyl that covered the two seats in the front.

"That's his storm cellar. Doris has been buryin' it for weeks now," Bobbie Joe explained as he came to a stop in front of the house.

"There's nothing wrong with a woman helping outside," Jimmy said.

"Yeah, but she does it all for that lazy bastard, and even asked me to come and help her shovel so she could get it done. I ain't shoveling dirt for no piece of tail, not for hers, anyways." Bobbie Joe looked at his watch. "Damn, it's 10:30 already. He's gonna try to get us to stay for lunch."

"I'll try to hurry. I have other places I need to be, too," Jimmy said. The panel at the top of his pager blinked where he had received a message. He pulled the pager from his jacket and checked it. The lighted panel displayed his home phone number. The note from Rachel read, "Buy a nanny so we can have some baby goats." He changed the indicator to vibrate so he'd know immediately when he received the next message.

Jimmy heard a loud bang and felt Bobbie Joe's truck shake from a solid impact. They jumped out to see what had happened. A large Billy goat with 15-inch horns had rammed the side of the pick-up. The goat's black hair stood on end down his spine. He appeared agitated and staggered around as if he were drunk. The goat turned away as Bobbie Joe cussed and kicked at it. It waddled off, dragging testicles the size of cantaloupes. The swollen organs caused the goat to run in a shuffling, bow-legged manner that reminded Jimmy of Bobbie Joe.

A voice shouted at the goat, and a filthy old man in Big Smith overalls chased after it. "Don't pay ole Billy any mind. He just got bit on the cods again by another cottonmouth. Happens to that rascal every time the nannies come in heat. Once that Billy starts chasin' tail, he quits payin' attention and forgets all about them damned snakes."

"That has got to be Claudie Walker," Jimmy said to Bobbie Joe.

"Yup," Bobbie Joe said. "Claudie, this here is Jimmy Lee. He's a math teacher from over at Delbert. He wants to buy a goat, and I told him you probably had a nanny to sell."

"Well, I got those two nannies right there on the front porch. I'll sell you either one of them for fifty dollars, or both of them for a hundred and twenty."

"He's a math teacher, Claudie, so he can add. You ain't gonna get away with that shit today. Sides, they's only one goat on that porch," Bobbie Joe said.

Claudie Walker looked at the porch and cursed. "Doris, run that damned nanny out here." He looked at Jimmy and said, "Damned goat loves to watch TV. Don't know why. The damn chickens are always roostin' on the antenna, so you can't get a picture worth lookin' at anyways."

"I reckon it's the sound, Claudie." The words and a stream of tobacco juice seemed to flow from Bobbie Joe's mouth at the same time. Then he wiped his mouth on his stained sleeve.

"Has either of those nannies been bred yet?" Jimmy asked Claudie.

"Don't know. They were both in heat earlier this week, and Billy was chasin' 'em all over the island." Claudie paused long enough to swat at a mosquito on his neck. "Till he got snake-bit, that is, so I don't know if he's done 'em any good or not. Doris likes watchin' 'em, gets her all worked up, if you know what I mean." Claudie looked at Jimmy and winked his blue eye as he continued to stare at something off to the left with his brown eye.

"Bobbie Joe, is that you?" came a woman's voice from the kitchen. She chased the goat out of the house and onto the front porch. Jimmy saw the woman and hoped she wasn't the one Bobbie Joe was humping.

The most striking feature about Doris was her tooth. It stood out like a chipmunk's would if it lost an incisor. The tooth was gold plated and looked dirty, as if she hadn't brushed it in a while. Later in the kitchen, when Jimmy got close enough, he could see her name inscribed on the tooth. It was spotless, and he came to the conclusion that Doris not only brushed that tooth, but polished it, although he doubted she ever flossed it, since it was the only tooth she had.

Doris had a potbelly bigger than her husband's, and her large mammaries swung like pendulums, always threatening to peek out from under her worn sweatshirt that said "Go Hogs" and seemed to ride half-way up her belly, exposing deep, red stretch-marks that colored the fat rolls of her abdomen. She wore an old faded pair of maroon pants, and she blew her nose on a dirty dishtowel as she grinned at Bobbie Joe Willie.

"Yeah, it's me," Bobbie Joe said.

"I'm makin' some chicken and dumplins. Y'all have to stay for lunch now, and I won't take no for an answer," she said.

"Ah, Doris, you know I love your dumplins, but Jimmy's gotta get back to town soon as we get that nanny loaded, and I'm already thirty minutes late getting the tavern open."

Jimmy checked his pager to make sure it was still on.

"You open that tavern late whenever it's convenient for ya, so I know better. Sides, dumplins will be done before you get that nanny loaded." She turned and went back into the house. Now both nannies stood out on the front porch.

"Well, which one do you want?" asked Claudie.

Jimmy walked up to the goats and made a serious attempt to look like he knew what he was doing. His fingers fondled the pager in his pocket. After he looked them up and down, Jimmy scratched his head and held his hand out to one of the goats. It bit his finger.

"Do either of them have a name?" Jimmy asked.

"Yeah, we call them Goat and Damned Goat," Claudie said.

Bobbie Joe Willie stood and stamped around like he had one foot in a red-ant hill. He finally eased up to Jimmy.

"Those dumplins will be ready 'fore we leave if you don't hurry."

"I'll take that white one, the Damned Goat. If she's not pregnant, can I bring her back and have her bred?"

"You sure can," said Claudie. "I'll personally see that she gets taken care of." He grabbed a rope hanging from a nail on the front porch. "Now let's get this bitch loaded so we can eat."

Bobbie Joe groaned like a man with stomach cramps. As Claudie reached for her, the nanny bolted into the house. It raced through the kitchen with Claudie Walker right behind it. Bobbie Joe and Jimmy chased Claudie through the house and into the kitchen, where Claudie stopped long enough to yell at Doris.

Doris stood in front of a wood cook stove, stirring a huge, old, rusted pot that steamed with something that looked like dumplins, with a bit of green color added. Flour was all over. On the counter— scratching in the flour—stood a large, white, Leghorn hen. Doris grabbed a stick of firewood from the pile along the wall to throw into the stove.

"I thought you was gonna put that Leghorn in the dumplin's," Claudie shouted.

"I was," Doris said, "but that Dominicker was sick and gonna die anyways."

Claudie ran on through the kitchen and out the back door with Bobbie Joe and Jimmy still trailing along behind. He jumped off the back porch and threw a noose around the nanny's neck. The nanny bucked and bleated and fought the rope like a rodeo calf. As Claudie eased his way, hand over hand, down the rope in an attempt to get closer to the nanny, the snake-bit Billy goat flashed by and rammed Claudie in the ass with those fifteen-inch horns, sending the old man in a rolling heap down the steep bank into the muddy water of the St. Francis River.

"Supper's ready," Doris called from the kitchen.

Bobbie Joe looked at Jimmy and said, "Have you paid for that goat yet?"

"Nope."

"Then let's get the hell out of here."

Jimmy didn't say a word as he turned and ran back through the kitchen. He had no desire to eat anything cooked where chickens and goats roamed at will. Bobbie Joe was right on his tail. The chicken still stood on the counter scratching at the bugs in the flour. Doris fell in behind them, running along behind Bobbie Joe as she screamed and cursed at him. She chased them through the house and out onto the front porch.

Jimmy cleared the porch with one leap and hit the ground running. He looked over his shoulder just in time to see Bobbie Joe trip and fall down the porch steps. The hounds bawled and scattered as Bobbie Joe interrupted their nap.

"Bobbie Joe Willie, I slave over that hot stove all mornin', and you come up here thinkin' you gonna get laid, but when my Claudie's here, you won't even stay for supper. You son of a bitch. I oughta kill your sorry ass."

Claudie Walker had released the nanny, got away from the Billy, and run through the kitchen and out on the front porch in time to hear what Doris had said. "You been humpin' Bobbie Joe? Where's my shotgun? I'll kill him for you." Claudie turned and ran back into the house.

Doris chased Claudie Walker back through the front door. Jimmy could hear her screaming at Claudie inside the cabin as he grabbed Bobbie Joe by the arm

"Can you make it to the truck?"

"Yeah, but you'll have to drive," Bobby Joe said.

They stumbled along, not realizing till it was too late they had staggered within range of a brilliantly colored game rooster who charged, trying to flog them with his inch-long spurs. The cock hit the end of his tether without reaching them and fell backwards. The iridescent plumage on his neck flared to make him look ferocious. Jimmy thought of Bull Anderson.

After he placed Bobbie Joe in the truck, Jimmy ran around, jumped in, and cranked on the starter. The engine came to life and he pulled it into gear. In the rear-view mirror, Jimmy saw Claudie Walker run onto the front porch with his shotgun and take aim at the truck. Doris came out of the house behind him, and with a stick of firewood hit Claudie over the head. Claudie fell to the ground as the shotgun discharged in the direction of the game roosters. Some pellets hit the bird that tried to flog them, and it started flopping about uncontrollably at the end of its tether. Jimmy smiled as he thought of Doris adding another rooster to her dumplins.

He jammed the accelerator to the floor and hit the levee road going as fast as he dared without tearing the bottom out of Bobbie Joe's truck. They'd been gone about five minutes before either of them spoke.

"Don't guess I'll be humpin' Doris anymore."

"I'd rather hump that nanny," Jimmy said. "I've never been shot at before."

"It don't hurt," Bobbie Joe said.

"My son's gonna be disappointed."

"We could always run up to Puxico. They have an auction every Saturday at noon, and always have goats there. Takes a couple hours round trip, so I doubt you could be back in time for what you gotta do today. But I'll go with you if you'd like, and we can drop your goat off at your house on the way back. Seems like the least I could do after getting you shot at. I may even buy a couple goats for next week's cookout."

The pager began to vibrate in Jimmy's pocket. In the excitement, he'd forgotten Gayle. After looking at the lighted display and recognizing her number, he put the device back down on the seat without checking the message.

"You need to call home? We can stop at the tavern if you want."

"I can call her back later," Jimmy said.

"Let's stop anyways. I need a six pack for the trip."

After stopping by the Red Onion Tavern to fill a cooler with cold beer, they finally pulled out on the paved road, and with Bobbie Joe Willie nursing a Budweiser, they turned to go to the livestock auction at Puxico, Missouri.

***

Returning from Puxico with three nanny goats and a kid—two of the nannies stayed with Bobbie Joe—Jimmy felt good about what he had done. Clayton was ecstatic about his new pets and had already learned the nanny would not be milked.

Rachel had helped Clayton pen the goats up in the small barn out in the pasture while Bobbie Joe took Jimmy back to Red Onion to get his truck. After eating supper, Clayton had bathed, and then fell asleep on the couch. Jimmy carried him to his room and tucked him in. When he returned, the den was empty and the television was still on. Rachel was taking a shower.

Jimmy sat and thought about what happened that day. Gayle had paged him three times before she finally quit. Tomorrow was Sunday, and Bull would be returning from Memphis.

Rachel came out of the bathroom brushing her long locks of wet hair. She wore a peach colored camisole with tap pants that barely covered her ass. Her breasts moved freely under the sheer fabric that hid nothing. Her figure narrowed down to twenty inches at her waist, giving her an hourglass outline. After she came and sat down in the floor at his feet, with her back toward him, she handed him the brush over her shoulder.

"Would you do this for me?" she asked.

"Have you been going to the tanning beds?"

"Yeah. Could you tell?"

"You look great. I can't wait to check out those tan lines," Jimmy said.

She laughed. "You know I never have tan lines. I lay nude."

He gently stroked her hair. She tilted her head back. Her eyes closed as she relaxed.

"I got shot at today," Jimmy said.

Rachel jerked forward, pulling the brush from Tommy's hand as it remained caught in her hair. "What did you say?"

"I got shot at. I went with Bobbie Joe Willie to Claudie Walker's to buy a goat. Bobbie's been seeing Claudie's wife, and Claudie figured it out while we were there."

"Were either of you hurt?" Rachel had turned and now sat with one knee up against her chest, her arm resting on the leg of her husband.

"Naw. Claudie missed us and hit one of his fighting roosters. I think Doris, his wife, the one Bobbie Joe was seeing, I think she hit him over the head with a stick of stove wood just in time." They shared a laugh.

"You don't need to go around those people anymore, Jimmy."

"I been thinking, about this 'doing right because it's right,' and not for fear of punishment. After Claudie shot at us, Bobbie Joe said he wouldn't be seeing Doris anymore. I just remembered thinking if he'd done the right thing from the beginning, none of that would have happened."

Rachel snuggled up closer to Tommy's legs and ran her fingers down the top of his thigh. "I know we've argued about this over Clayton. But if he learns to do the right thing for the right reason, that might never happen with him."

"Please don't preach at me about this. I'm giving in," Jimmy said.

She rested her cheek against his leg.

Jimmy took the brush again and gently stroked her hair. He wanted to tell her what had happened. He wanted to tell her he had done the right thing because he loved her; because he didn't want to lose the moments like this. He even tried to convince himself that he was not afraid of Bull Anderson. That the only reason he didn't go over and fuck Gayle was because he loved his wife and didn't want to lose her. But he knew that was a lie. At least, yesterday, it had been a lie.

The Sheriff of Jester County

Sheriff Wilson Underwood's pistol went off in its holster just as he tried to sit down behind his desk. The bullet—a hollow-point .357—lodged in the block wall across the room. Within seconds after the discharge, Jack Ditta, the Delbert City Marshall, burst into the office with his pistol drawn. Wilson sat in the floor against the back wall trying to shuck his smoking jeans.

"Are you all right?" Ditta said as he rushed across the room to the sheriff's side.

"Huh," Wilson said.

No prisoners or jail trustees were injured, but everyone who entered the jail for the next six weeks had to walk by and look at the hole in the wall, including the county judge, Joe Mack Arnold, and the Jester County quorum court. The court funded the jail and the sheriff's office. After the incident, they passed a resolution encouraging Wilson to retire the weapon, though they refused to give him any extra money in the jail budget to buy a replacement. After six months of legal wrangling and political bickering, Wilson gave up on getting a new pistol.

One afternoon, nearly nine months after the pistol discharged, Wilson finished his shift and went home for the evening. After he walked into the kitchen and kissed his wife, he asked about Amy.

"She's been in her room all day," Carol said.

"You think the lock's a mistake?" Wilson dipped his finger into the bowl of cake batter Carol had left unattended.

"I think it'll take some getting used to. She's outgrown us." Carol swatted at his hand.

Wilson walked into the living room where he removed his holster and tossed it on the coffee table at the end of the couch. The gun exploded. Marked by a furrow of splintered wood scorched by flame from the gun's muzzle, the bullet's path led to a hole in the wall the size of a nickel. Wilson's ears rang from the sound of the blast, and although his wife's screams sounded as if they came from the end of a long tunnel, he heard the startled gasp of his daughter in the next room as if she'd whispered her last breath in his ear.

He stumbled into the hall and tried the locked door to Amy's room. The size of a silver dollar, the hole in the sheetrock marked where the expanded bullet had passed through the hall. Wilson knew the massive tissue damage a hollow point bullet caused; he'd seen more than one gunshot wound during his career. Like so many times before, while executing and serving warrants, he stepped back and tried to raise his foot to kick open the door. Instead, he leaned against the wall slumped over like a drunk, unable to stand, or fall, or move. The distant screaming of his wife dissipated for a moment as she left the hall and then returned from the kitchen with a key they kept stored in a drawer. She attacked the lock and finally opened the door.

Wilson saw his daughter. Amy had dropped the book she held, and her tiny, white hand lay half off the bed with her slender fingers extended–as if she waited for someone to read her future in her palm. With her eyes closed and a trace of a smile on her face, she appeared to be caught in a dream. But Wilson saw the crimson around her on the sheets; he smelled the fecal odor of a gut-shot, and he heard the sound of his own voice.

She was his only daughter, and he'd tried to forgive himself. His wife didn't. Carol blamed Wilson for Amy's death, for the embarrassment of the investigations that came afterward, for the closed casket at the delayed funeral—a result of the autopsy that followed weeks after Amy's death. She blamed him for their friends who came by to wish them well but wanted to see the hole in the wall where the bullet went through.

At the next Quorum Court meeting, a resolution funding the purchase of a new pistol for the sheriff passed without discussion.

After taking their daughter to the hospital, Wilson and Carol never opened the door to the bedroom again. The investigators with the State Police had sealed the room for evidence and ordered Wilson not to patch the hole until they finished their investigation. A year later the case was closed, and Carol left, taking $500,000—half of the settlement they received from the gun manufacturer. As part of the divorce settlement, they agreed to hire ServiceMaster to come in and clean the room. Neither of them had the courage to do it themselves.

Wilson never patched the holes in the walls.

The first Christmas without them, Wilson bought and decorated a tree. But coming home to an empty house and a tree with no presents depressed him. At the Belk's store over at Success, Wilson bought presents for Amy. He wrapped and placed them under the tree and even hung her old stocking, with her name stitched on the front by her mother, on the fireplace mantle. During the first years he bought small items: dolls and dollhouses, little stuffed penguins, albums like Prince's *Purple Rain* and Madonna's *Like a Virgin*, posters of *Top Gun* and *St. Elmo's Fire*. Anything he could find that Amy had shown an interest in, he bought.

The years passed and he realized Amy would be maturing, and he tried to imagine his daughter as a young woman becoming interested in boys and wanting make-up, needing bras and tampons, and graduating high school. In 1989, the year she would have graduated, he bought a gold graduation ring with an emerald birthstone and her name etched on the side. A purple, sequined prom dress and a small bottle of perfume completed the ensemble that Wilson bought for Amy's senior year. The ring and the perfume he wrapped and placed in the stocking that he stuffed on Christmas Eve. The dress he wrapped and placed under the tree with a hundred dollar Maybelline kit that included lipstick, mascara, eyeliner, and every shade of blush imaginable. Each year the presents remained under the tree until the New Year, and all evidence of the desolate holidays could be removed.

Wilson didn't know what to do with the gifts—to unwrap and return the items for a refund would ruin the illusion. He moved the wrapped packages to the attic where they sat and collected dust. He tried to imagine Amy a year older every holiday season, and he tried to guess what she'd want. As the years passed, Amy's presents filled the attic.

***

Wilson didn't see the armadillo until Earl Montgomery pointed at it. Propped against the last meter, on the corner of Main and Pruitt in the spot that Earl always saved for him, the dead creature held a beer bottle between its three-toed paws. A cigarette hung from the side of its mouth, and its long snout supported a pair of Blues Brothers sunglasses secured by a wire that ran behind its wheat-shaped ears. Earl waved and Wilson nodded his head in acknowledgement as he drove on past, eased up to the curb, and got out. With a spade he kept behind his seat, Wilson tossed the armadillo carcass in the back of his truck. He suspected his newest deputy, Steve Finnegan, was responsible for the armadillos that kept turning up on the town square. Finnegan had a strange fascination with dead things and had become a grave liability during the current election, an election Wilson had to win to receive his full pension.

Leaning against the shovel, Wilson watched the traffic and wondered how a town square as small as Delbert's could become so crowded on Fridays. At the Main and Court street intersection, from noon till one, you could count on spending fifteen minutes trying to get through, unless Earl was there. In knee boots and a faded L.L. Bean cap, Earl had waded into the crossing, just as he had on the last Friday of the month for the past twenty odd years. He wore a faded green goose-down vest over a red flannel shirt; he looked like an olive stuffed with a pimento. A bull sprig whistle hung from the lanyard around his neck along with a black P.S. Olt duck call made in Pekin, Illinois. The lanyard held over fifty U.S. Fish and Wildlife Service leg-bands that Earl had removed from the ducks he'd taken during his years as a guide in the Hatchie Coon Bottoms of the St. Francis River.

Etta Coffman pulled up to the intersection in her gray 1972 Chevy Impala and stopped as Earl held his hand out and blew on the whistle. "I knew you'd be here, Earl," she said as she waved a bottle of her homemade muscadine wine out the window of her car. "You chill this till tomorrow night."

Earl grinned at her and waved the traffic to a stop. He walked to her car and took the old Boone's Farm bottle with the label removed and stuffed it in the front pocket of his vest. After he sprinted back to the middle of the intersection, he blew on his whistle and stopped a Craighead Electric service truck to allow Etta to ease on through. Wilson could see Earl's head over the top of a car as it drove by, and he wondered just how tall the old man really was.

Although the leaves of the white oaks that lined the square had taken on an October hue, the noontime sun in Delbert still felt hot, so Wilson tossed the shovel in the truck-bed and walked into Campbell's Café. He saw Ruben Johnson sitting at a window waiting for Jenny to bring his plate-lunch special. Ruben pointed at Earl as Wilson made his way toward him. Wilson looked toward the intersection. Earl had waived a high-water four-wheel drive to a stop. The man driving the truck pointed at the bottle of wine sticking half out of Earl's vest. Then he offered him a beer. The old man refused.

"Earl never drinks when he's on duty," Wilson said as he made his way to the table.

"He's off his medicine again," Ruben said

"Now, you don't know that." Wilson pulled back a chair and sat down.

"That's what everybody says. So I guess there's some truth to it," Ruben said.

"Well, I know one thing. I'll bet when that New Madrid earthquake hits he'll be out there trying to direct traffic. If there is any." Wilson looked around the diner for Jenny.

"No California scientist is gonna guess the day of the next big earthquake," Ruben said. He took a sip of coffee and looked out the pane-glass window at Earl. "But who knows. He got his last one right. Nearly cancelled the World Series over it."

"Besides, Earl only directs traffic on the last Friday of the month. The earthquake is scheduled for December second," Wilson said.

"Predicted, not scheduled. Earl might come in handy when that quake hits," Ruben said. He reached for a menu and handed it to Wilson.

In an attempt to look like any other citizen, Wilson wore dark blue Wranglers with a white Oxford shirt. He never wore the standard issue uniform he required all his deputies to wear. A badge hung from his belt, a style favored by the investigators who worked for the Arkansas State Police. 1990 was an election year, and October marked the final frantic days of campaigning before the citizens of Jester County cast their ballots on the first Tuesday of November.

50

"He's gonna get himself killed out there one of these days, Wilson."

"Earl's been directing traffic down here for years now. There's never been an accident while he was on duty. I wish I had that kind of record."

The sounds of the busy café, contested conversation between friends and forks on china, framed the silence at the table until Jenny walked up with a plate of food and a pot of coffee. She topped off their cups and asked, "Who gets the black-eyed peas?"

"Put those peas right here, young lady."

"You get your own peas, Sheriff," Jenny said as she smiled and set the plate in front of Ruben. She looked up and saw Earl through the window. "Earl's directing traffic again. Rent'll be due next week. He's consistent as a calendar."

"Election's just around the corner, Jenny. You registered to vote?"

"Always vote for you, Wilson. What do you want for lunch?"

"Give me some meatloaf, mashed potatoes, and black-eyed peas with a glass of sweet tea."

"Cornbread or roll?"

"Bring me both," Wilson said.

Before Jenny could write down his order, Wilson asked, "How old are your twins now, Jenny?"

"Thirteen going on twenty-one, if you know what I mean. I gotta meet with Mrs. White for a teacher's conference today. I know that damned Mooney Marrs is still bitching about them hexing Mooney Jr.," she replied just before she scurried off, filling coffee cups as she worked her way back to the kitchen.

If he gave the presents to Jenny's girls, Wilson could empty the room upstairs. The attic at his house now overflowed with wrapped presents—some he had stored for twelve years. But Wilson didn't believe he could let them go. At least one room in the house was still full.

Buck Donnick walked in the door of Campbell's Café followed by Jess McCord, his campaign manager. The Jester County Republicans had finally nominated a candidate for sheriff, and the county was having its first contested November election in years.

Buck looked around the room at the potential voters and let his eyes settle on the table of Wilson Underwood, his opponent for the election next Tuesday. Buck smiled, removed the white Resistol hat from his head, and immediately began working his way toward Wilson, stopping to shake hands and solicit votes along the way. Jess McCord walked to the bulletin board and hung a campaign poster, then left a big stack of business cards at the cash register.

"Hello, Wilson. Figured you'd be in here." Buck offered his hand to the man whose job he hoped to take. After a moment of hesitation, Wilson shook it.

"They don't allow no soliciting in here, Buck. Don't make me arrest you before the election." Wilson forced a laugh after he spoke the words.

"Now, that'd be just like a politician. Arrest your opponent a week before the election so you could say you were tough on crime." Buck stood in front of the table, still shaking the sheriff's hand. "I hope you'd release me before the earthquake. I doubt that old jail will still be standing afterwards." In a pair of pleated gray trousers with a sharp crease, and a white linen shirt that hung loose around his shoulders, Buck flashed like silk when he moved. He kept a small tablet in his shirt pocket to take notes while campaigning. The gray hair had disappeared shortly before he announced for the election. Delilah Marrs, Delbert's only beautician, swore the color he used was subject to client privileges.

He looked back at the sheriff and said, "There's old Earl Montgomery out there breaking the law again. Why don't you go arrest him before he gets himself run over?"

Buck claimed Wilson refused to enforce the law by allowing Earl Montgomery to direct traffic, and by allowing Etta Coffman to have a still. Buck also accused Archie Snell of murdering his wife, and Wilson of covering it up by refusing to order an autopsy. The headline across the top of Donnick's campaign posters read, "Sheriff Wilson Underwood is soft on crime." A picture of Joe Don Baker as Buford Pusser—the famous strong-armed McNairy County lawman of *Walking Tall* fame—occupied the top right-hand corner, and the words under the picture read, "We don't need this type of law enforcement in our county." Across the bottom of the poster was a picture of Don Knotts as Barney Fife, with a pistol in one hand and the other in his pocket fumbling for his bullet. The caption read, "But do we have to settle for this?"

"Why don't you have a seat, Buck, and let's have some lunch together. Call the war off for thirty minutes. Hell, we can make plans for dealing with the earthquake if you like."

"Sorry, Sheriff, I got campaigning to do. You wouldn't interrupt your lunch to arrest a man for campaigning, would you?" Buck turned, not giving the sheriff a chance to reply, and started working his way toward the back of the café to the table where Jess McCord sat waiting with Larry Cole, the newest member of the Republican party. Wilson rose from his seat. Ruben reached a hand over and placed it on Wilson's wrist.

"Let it go, Wilson."

"If Archie Snell ever gets his hands on him, I'll have a real murder to investigate."

"Let's just hope he didn't see Etta give Earl that bottle," Ruben said. "He'd have a hey-day with that."

Wilson pulled some money out of his shirt pocket. "She can give it away all day, as long as she don't sell it."

"I'll get this," Ruben said.

"Can't nobody buy me lunch. You know that."

"I'm chair of your re-election committee. We can write it off as a campaign expense."

"Don't let that bastard see you," Wilson said as he gestured toward Buck.

"Get back to work and let me worry about this. There hasn't been a Republican sheriff in Jester County since Reconstruction," Ruben said with a grin.

"Yeah, and it'd be my luck he'd be the first." Wilson sat back down. He pulled a tin of Prince Albert tobacco from his hip and a package of Joker wrappers from his shirt pocket. After he licked and formed the wrapper, he tapped the tobacco out of the can and rolled the cigarette into a perfect form.

Ruben offered his lighter.

"Just go do your job. You're a legend in this county, Wilson. You'll be sheriff for as long as you want," Ruben said.

Wilson walked out of the café and got into his truck. Instead of accepting the new patrol car the county always bought the sheriff after each election, Wilson had rigged his pick-up with a radio and lights so he could drive it on patrol. The number of deputies available to patrol the county roads became an issue in every election, so he hired Steve Finnegan as an extra deputy with the unspent money. The only qualified applicant for the job, Finnegan had been certified as a police officer at the academy in Camden, Arkansas, but his application with the Arkansas State Police never got past the personality test.

Going east on Main and crossing the tracks by the Melon Grocer's building, Wilson headed out to Wild Hog Road. He passed one of Beaver Howell's cut rice fields full of snow geese. More of the birds circled in the air overhead as they tried to find a bare spot to land. They reminded him of bees circling a hive.

He pulled to the side of the road and watched and wondered why birds could migrate thousands of miles every winter and never get lost, but people have to be directed around the town square. What causes that first bird to get up and fly off towards the south? What causes all the other birds to get up and follow along? He wondered how many landed on some hunter's kitchen table; how many would live to make the trip back north, and which one would lead the way back to Canada in the spring.

There were so many answers he didn't have to so many questions he wanted to ask. Every day as sheriff was a quest for answers. Understanding why people did things was the key to solving any crime. Wilson knew Earl saw the counselors at the Crowley's Ridge Counseling unit over at Success on a regular basis, and that he took medication to cope with a personality disorder. But Wilson had never given a thought before today to why Earl wore hip boots when he directed traffic. And why always the last Friday of the month?

The toughest questions to answer, however, were always the ones he asked of himself. Why couldn't he choose cornbread over a roll at lunch? He liked cornbread best. Why did he have to prepare the county for an earthquake that would never happen? Why did he have to be the first sheriff to have a Republican opponent in November? Why didn't he get rid of that pistol the first time it misfired?

Wilson looked at his watch and remembered the three o'clock appointment he had with Delilah Marrs. If anyone in the county knew why Earl directed traffic, she would. Wilson had solved more than one crime with information Delilah overheard at the beauty shop. But even Delilah had her limits. She would help Wilson with any gossip she heard, but refused to admit she had dyed Buck Donnick's hair.

"Gossip isn't subject to client privilege," she had said.

Wilson started his truck, and the sound flushed the flock of geese. As he turned around to head back to town, the solid white cloud of birds lifted from the ground as one living mass.

***

"Hello Wilson, I wondered if you were gonna make it," Delilah Marrs said, as he walked through the door of God's House of Beauty Salon. Delilah was the wife of the Reverend Mooney Marrs who pastored the church next door.

"You give me one of those Butch haircuts again and I'll lock you up, Delilah."

"Ah, Wilson, you're sexy with a Butch."

"I bet you're on Buck's payroll." Wilson sat down in the middle chair. Delilah threw a sheet around him and pinned it behind his neck. He felt her large breasts against his shoulders. Delilah always earned the five dollar tip he gave her.

"I already shaved today, thank God."

"I wouldn't cut your throat, no matter how much Buck pays me. And Buck knows that. How about a manicure? I won't tell anybody."

"Just a haircut today."

"Then let's get that mop looking decent. How's the new dispatcher working out?" She picked up a comb and parted his hair.

"Better than our new deputy. I guess you've heard what Finnegan did with that Conley girl's panties?"

"That girl who committed suicide?"

Wilson nodded his head.

"Be still." Delilah pinched his chin and tilted his head forward. "Yeah, don't remind me. You should have fired that sick bastard."

"Don't let the preacher hear you talk like that."

"Well, he's one, too. Why didn't you fire Finnegan?"

"Can't fire a deputy this close to an election. He'd go straight to Buck with a bunch of lies, and I'd have no time for damage control."

"Switch him over to dog catcher. That's a county position, isn't it?" Delilah turned Wilson around so she could talk to him in the mirror.

"We need to fill it, too. I shoveled up another damned armadillo today on the city square. All dressed up like Saturday night, and I'd bet anything Finnegan's the one doing it. He's gonna catch leprosy handling those things."

"Have you seen him do it?"

"Some things you just know."

"You should have sent him in on those Posse idiots."

Without a vest, Wilson had kicked a door in after an hour-long siege with members of the Posse Comitatus, a militant anti-tax group of white survivalists and skinheads. The two occupants of the house died from his shotgun blasts after he burst through the door. The rest of the Posse moved to Idaho shortly thereafter.

The Jester County Republicans claimed Wilson had a death wish. Buck Donnick had told more than one voter that Wilson would never have taken such a risk when his daughter was still alive. But for Wilson, going through that door was easy.

"What do you know about Earl Montgomery?"

Delilah fussed over the sheriff's hair. After taking a few extra moments, she spoke, in a slow and deliberate manner, as if she carefully chose each word. "I cut his hair once about ten years ago. He's bald now. That's probably why he wears that cap all the time. "

"Why does he wear those stupid hip boots when he's directing traffic?"

With a small pair of scissors, she trimmed the hair in Wilson's ears. "No one ever asked that before."

56

"He got a thing for Etta Coffman? She gave him a bottle of her wine today and told him to keep it iced for tomorrow night."

"Miss Etta? She makes some damned good wine. Mooney used it once for communion. Pissed off half the church." Delilah spun the chair around and started on the other side of the sheriff's head. "I never noticed the hip boots. No one's ever stopped him, or asked him why, so far as I know." She spun the chair around and looked at Wilson to make sure both sides of his trim were even. "So, Miss Etta got a date."

"I just hope Buck didn't see it. I'm sick of him telling everyone he's gonna raid her still when he's elected."

"Her husband's been dead five years come December. About time that old woman moved on."

The call came over the portable radio Wilson carried whenever he left his truck.

Delilah stopped combing his hair when they heard the squawk and the voice of the new dispatcher.

"501, there's been a pedestrian struck by a train downtown." Wilson fumbled under the cape for his mike.

"This is 501. Do they have an ID on the pedestrian?"

"No, sir. The body's tore up pretty bad."

"You can pay me tomorrow," Delilah said as she removed the cape and watched him bolt for the door. "Be careful, Wilson."

Wilson saw flashing lights as he approached the tracks just off the town square. Jack Ditta, the City Marshall, was already there, along with Collins Kilgore, a State Trooper, and Deputy Steve Finnegan.

A dead-end line where the railroad repair crews stored their machinery was usually empty, but now, it bristled with equipment. The arms of the booms reminded Wilson of scorpion tails lumbering above the open cars filled with new crossties. He cursed as he drove up to the tracks. If the tie gang had been working, the train would have been stalled. But the gang worked eight days on and six days off. Their break had started two days ago.

The prediction of a major earthquake along the New Madrid Fault resulted in a flurry of activity along the rail lines in Jester County. The Union Pacific had brought in an engineer from

California to shore up as many of the bridges as they could. The tie gangs and rail gangs seemed permanently stationed in the county, and Wilson had dealt with many complaints about the long delays of traffic while the gangs made their repairs.

The sirens of an ambulance and another state police unit announced their arrival on the other side of the tracks. Mack Harbor, the county's other State Police officer, must have been coming on duty when the report of the accident came over the radio. Both vehicles parked between the train and the Melon Building. The rolling red lights of the ambulance and the flashing blue lights of the patrol car seemed to animate the mural on the building behind them, creating a carnival atmosphere that reminded Wilson of the Earthquake Festival the city had held back in April. The lights from the rides and carnival stands lit up the whole downtown area. He had won two stuffed penguins at the shooting range—Amy had collected penguins. Wilson took them home and placed them on her bed where they sat until he wrapped them for Christmas.

On the ground, a couple hundred yards to the south, lay a white cloth. Finnegan, Kilgore, and Ditta cast about, searching the area along the tracks. Wilson reached for his radio.

"504, this is 501. I'm north of you, back up the tracks. What have you got down there?"

"A stump of a body. We're walking both sides of the track trying to find the rest."

"You figured out who this is?"

"Not yet, boss."

"I'll be right there."

Wilson got out of his truck and walked up to the train. Vehicles lined the streets in both directions at the downtown intersections. He'd send Finnegan to redirect the traffic. Steve couldn't screw that up, he thought.

As he eased along the tracks, Wilson bent to look under the cars and between the wheels and axles. He saw an occasional dark spot of blood, but didn't see anything else until he looked ahead. A pale hand stuck out between two axles. Wilson stopped. The hand looked white as cotton. With fingers bent slightly and pressed together, the palm skyward, it appeared as if someone had reached

58

out, trying to catch a drop of rain. He approached the severed appendage and knelt on the sharp gray ballast that served as the foundation for the train tracks. Neatly trimmed, the manicured nails gave the hand a feminine look. Wilson remembered Delilah's comment that she wouldn't tell anyone if he got a manicure that morning and the way she acted when he asked her about Earl. Earl's hands had looked small while directing traffic that morning, but this hand was not small, and no calluses marked the palm or fingers. Earl hadn't worked in years, though, and his hands would look small against that large frame of his.

Along the outside of the rail, almost a foot away from the hand, Wilson saw the bull sprig whistle.

If he'd arrested Earl that morning, the man would still be alive. If he'd thrown that pistol away the first time it went off, his daughter would have graduated from high school; he would still be married, and he wouldn't be living alone, storing prom dresses, graduation rings, and years worth of Christmas presents in his attic. Wilson had botched his own death—killing the two Posse members before they could even get off a shot. His miserable attempt at suicide had resulted in the death of two men who might have surrendered, and his coronation as a hero, a term he loathed because of the lie it hid.

"Wrap it up in this," Buck Donnick said. He had walked up behind Wilson and handed him a white plastic garbage bag. Wilson stood to take the bag and shake it open. Then he crouched and eased around the hand like he was about to grab a live rattlesnake. He pinched the end of one of the fingers and pulled it out from between the axles of the boxcar. The wheels of the train had severed the wrist mid-way between the hand and elbow. Feathers from the goose down vest Earl wore that morning matted the bloody stump. Wilson placed the remains in the sack.

"I reckon we should mark that spot," Wilson said.

"Spray some paint there." Buck gave Wilson a can of orange spray paint.

"I guess you'll have fun with this one," Wilson said as he painted the area where he found the hand.

"What do you mean?"

"If I'd arrested him this morning, like you said, this wouldn't have happened."

"Arrested him for what? I'm not here politicking, Wilson."

"I didn't think you knew the difference," Wilson said.

"I showed up to help. I am a first responder with the fire department, you know."

"How could you have made those posters, Buck? You drug my daughter into this campaign."

"Jess did that. I didn't want to use them, Wilson. But he already had them up."

"You can take the goddamned things down. There's no need."

They heard a whoop from up the tracks and both men looked toward the noise. Deputy Finnegan was bent over, looking under the train. When he stood, he held up a severed leg. "It ain't so bad," he said. "No worse than a rare steak. Just needs a little hot sauce." Holding the bloody end away from his body, he laughed out loud and bit the knee.

"Please, tell me he didn't just do that," Buck said.

"You sure you wanna be sheriff, Buck?" Wilson handed him the white plastic bag, then began walking up the tracks toward his deputy. Still pretending to gnaw on the leg, Finnegan looked up from his mock feast just as the sheriff came within reach. Wilson planted his feet in the loose ballast and rolled his shoulders and hips, locking his elbow at the perfect moment when the blow struck Finnegan between the eyes. The deputy fell next to the tracks and lay still; his eyes closed, his fingers twitching.

Wilson turned and stared at his own feet as he walked back down the tracks. He laughed and shook his head, then bent over to pick up the intact bottle of muscadine wine.

Wilson spoke into his radio. "Jack, have y'all got this under control?"

"We're almost finished, Wilson. We found Earl's head down here with his wallet. Mike Dickerson, the UP man is here now, and he has some more he needs to do."

"Make sure the medics look at Finnegan before they leave, then send him home. I'm gone." Wilson looked at Buck. Buck looked away.

With the wine cradled in his arm like an orphan child, Wilson walked to his truck. He drove to Earl's house to see if anyone was there. Earl lived alone, but Wilson knew the old man had family somewhere. The small brick home looked tidy, and the grounds had been edged and trimmed and recently mowed. After he knocked on the door and received no answer, Wilson walked around the house and checked all the windows and doors to make sure they were locked. Once word got out that Earl was dead, someone might try to break in. The manicured lawn stopped at the edge of the steep bank of a creek that bordered the backyard. A well-worn trail led down the bank to the east. Wilson knew the creek ran right behind Etta Coffman's.

A few minutes later, he pulled up onto the bridge over Nickel Creek and stopped. If he got out and looked, Wilson knew he'd find the path that led from Earl's to Ms. Coffman's back door and the spot where Earl waded across the creek. So that answered the question of the hip boots, but why direct traffic? Why on the last Friday of the month? Maybe why we do things isn't anyone else's business. Maybe peace of mind is all the motivation anyone needs for what we do, even those things that seem insane to those around us. But Wilson couldn't think of any good reason to keep storing those presents in his attic. The Department of Human Services over at Success always collected presents from the community for the poor children in the county. That might be a good way to get rid of the gifts.

He eased across the bridge and pulled into Etta Coffman's driveway. The home, a simple frame structure, had recently been covered with white vinyl siding. Three rows of grape vines hung from trellises in the lot next to the house. The thick-skinned muscadines grew wild in most parts of Arkansas, made excellent jelly, and a sweet but potent wine. Wilson didn't know what he would say to the woman. This part of his job had always been difficult. He wondered if being told of the death of a loved one was as bad as being there to see it happen, or as bad as having to deliver the message. It certainly wasn't as bad as moving on afterwards. Holding the bottle of wine in his left arm, Wilson walked through the gate and up the ancient sidewalk. He climbed the steps and stopped in front of another closed door.

Poverty Line

Jenny sat in a chair positioned outside Mrs. White's classroom and waited for her conference with her daughters' teacher. She looked at her watch. Five more minutes.

As her twins had grown older, they began to ask Jenny about things they didn't know or understand, things that Jenny could only try to explain: why do women wear bras and girls don't? Why are we the only twins in school? What's a tampon? Do you ever douche? Why is Mooney Jr. black when both of his parents are white?

But the question Jenny was most prepared to answer came early, and proved the hardest to explain.

"Why don't we have a daddy like everybody else?"

Jenny had paused for a moment before she answered, and then she forgot her carefully rehearsed words. "Of course you had a daddy, but he died before you were born."

"Were you married?" Dana asked.

"No. We never married," Jenny said.

"But you said we should wait till we're married before we have sex," Donna said.

"Yes, I did. But I didn't, and it was a good thing, because your daddy died before we could marry." Jenny cringed as she lied to her daughters. Their daddy never even knew he was to be a father, and the topic of marriage never came up on their only night together. But the girls weren't old enough to know or understand what had happened. Her date with Randy White, the son of her favorite teacher, was a blind date, on Valentine's Day in 1978, that ended in casual sex. Eight weeks later Jenny had missed her period, and Randy White had died—electrocuted in a freak accident at the Marmon plant in Delbert.

A chair creaked as it slid across the floor from within the classroom, and moments later, the door opened.

"Come on in, Jenny. I've been waiting for you," said Mrs. White. "I'm surprised you came."

"I don't know why. I haven't missed one of these conferences since my girls started kindergarten," Jenny said as she sat in the chair across from Mrs. White. "No one ever went to mine."

"I was wrong to speak to you the way I did at Campbell's that day," Mrs. White said. "But that was a long time ago. Years ago."

"Fourteen years. But not long enough to forget. You scared me. I watched your husband in court for the Children's Home all those years. I knew I couldn't afford a legal battle with you for my girls."

"We didn't want the girls. We thought you wanted money, and we didn't believe the baby, the twins, were Randy's."

"I heard you got a million dollars when you settled the lawsuit over Randy's death. The girls are thirteen years old, and I haven't asked you for one penny."

"We didn't quite get a million dollars. But we know the girls are Randy's," Mrs. White said. She sat with her hands clasped together, resting on the desk in front of her.

"I told you that at the café fourteen years ago. I thought we were gonna talk about school today."

"I want to talk about that, too," said Mrs. White. "I also have to inform you of the preparations the school district is making for this earthquake prediction by Iben Browning. Class has been cancelled that day, just in case, and we are handing out the *Red Cross Earthquake Survival Guide* and encouraging all school patrons to stock up on water, food, and medical supplies. That's all in this brochure." Mrs. White handed Jenny the pamphlet across the desk. "But there's really nothing else to discuss where school's concerned. They make *A's* in everything. Nothing in this classroom is even close to being a challenge for them. Since you took that Voodoo book away, they have even gotten along better with Mooney Jr."

Both women laughed. During the spring semester, her daughters took to school a voodoo book that Jenny had purchased at the Nu-2-U Flea Market. The girls, a pair of red-haired, green-eyed beauties, had cast a spell on Mooney Jr., and he went home sick. Of course, it didn't matter to the Reverend Marrs and his wife that ten other students also complained of stomach cramps after eating the fermented pineapple served in the cafeteria that day. Mooney Marrs

63

Sr. had requested prayer for Jenny and her twins the next Sunday in church and preached a fiery sermon about witchcraft, sorcery, Ouija Boards, and prejudice. Bull Anderson had refused to discipline the twins, so the school principal also made the prayer list at Mooney Marrs' church—out of alphabetical order and next to the names of Jenny and the twins.

"I never dreamed that book would cause so much trouble. I'm so sorry," Jenny said. She noticed a picture of a redheaded youth with dark eyes sitting on the teacher's desk.

"What are you doing with a picture of Dana?"

"That's not Dana, Jenny. That's Randy."

Jenny stood and leaned across the desk to get a better look at the picture. She sat back down with the picture in her hand. The picture wasn't of Dana; both girls had Jenny's green eyes. The eyes in the picture were brown.

"James and I want to acknowledge the girls as our granddaughters. We want to become a part of their lives. We'd like for you and the girls to spend the holidays, Thanksgiving and Christmas, with us. We've set aside a substantial trust for their college, if you'll let them have it."

Jenny stood up from her seat and walked toward the windows. She could imagine her girls playing in the yard, creating mischief, sitting in the corner next to the fence and casting spells on Mooney Jr., then coming home to the Whites' mansion.

"Why?" Jenny asked as she continued to stare out the window. "Why now?"

"You're a parent, Jenny. Only a parent can empathize with someone who loses a child."

"That's not good enough. I don't want to lose my daughters."

"We don't want to be parents, Jenny. But this is our only chance to be grandparents."

"If I say no, you'll just go to court and take them."

"After the way I treated you, you have every right to say no. But I believe you are a better person than that."

"Oh, now you're gonna say I'm a good person? How about all those times you called me a money-grubbing tramp? When you said I was a piece of trailer-trash that saw a chance for a monthly check when Randy died? You said that at the café, the day Glen had to run you off."

"Are you a perfect parent, Jenny?"

"This isn't about me," Jenny said.

"I knew I had made a mistake the day I left the café, a bad mistake. I was to retire three years ago, but I stayed, just to teach these girls. Let me show you something." Mrs. White opened the bottom drawer of her desk and pulled out a large scrapbook with ragged edges that overflowed with papers and memorabilia. "Move around here," she said as she pointed to a spot next to her chair. Jenny obediently moved her chair around next to her former teacher. Mrs. White opened the scrapbook to the first page.

Jenny looked at pictures taken of her twins when they were in kindergarten. Yellowed tape secured copies of their report cards to the opposite page. Mrs. White sat and flipped through page after page of the book, revealing to Jenny events in her twins' lives that happened at school—events even Jenny didn't know about.

"Here is Mr. Anderson's report from last spring when he talked to the girls about the spell they cast on Mooney Jr. He let me take this from his office so it wouldn't become a part of their permanent file. He wasn't gonna let me till I told him the girls were my granddaughters."

"You told him that? What gave you the right?"

"I was trying to help them, Jenny. Bull already knew of the relationship, and I didn't want anyone to come up and say they had practiced witchcraft later. You know how ridiculous the Reverend Marrs can be. Especially when it comes to how the children treat Delilah's son. He's the only black student we have in the entire county school system, and the children delight in tormenting him."

"How did Mr. Anderson know?"

"Jenny, they've talked about me up here worse than a dog for not acknowledging those girls. But I didn't think I could face you again after I was thrown out of the cafeteria. My husband and I have talked about this for years now. We will respect your decision, whatever that decision is. But we know we've made a terrible mistake. We have nothing left of Randy and watching these girls grow up and knowing they belonged to him—"

"My girls belong to me."

"I didn't mean that, Jenny, I promise. I meant, they were his biological children."

"Why are you willing to accept this all of a sudden? Without even asking for a paternity test? You were worried about me asking for money before. Are you trying to *buy* me now?"

"Look at that," Mrs. White said as she pointed to Randy's picture on her desk. "A paternity test can't give me proof any more positive than that. I don't think they could even do a test after all these years, and we don't want to know different. We want to take your word for it."

"How the hell are you gonna do this? You can't just announce in class tomorrow that Donna and Dana are your grandkids, and they will call you Grandma from now on instead of Mrs. White."

"No. I had planned to retire after this school year. But if you will let us do this, I will retire at the Christmas break. We would love to be able to spend Christmas with the girls."

Jenny wilted in her seat. She felt her world imploding as she saw herself alone in her house at Christmas, her girls at the White mansion, opening presents that Jenny could never afford to buy them. After a child reached a certain age, they could go before the court and ask to live with the person they wanted to be with. Jenny knew this from her youth at the Children's Home.

"Jenny, I meant with you—and the girls. We know you have no family. We don't just want to acknowledge the girls; we want you along with them. We thought we could all spend Thanksgiving together, spend some time getting to know each other, and then tell the girls at Christmas. If you've already made other plans, we can be flexible."

"I'd have to fix something to bring with us for Thanksgiving. I've always taught the girls you never go anywhere empty-handed."

"That would be fine. I'd love to try some of your cooking."

"You want a lot." Jenny sat and played with the hem of her blue skirt. She ran her fingers over the coffee stain from work that morning. "I need some time. I came today expecting trouble from you over the voodoo thing; I wasn't expecting this. You were my favorite teacher, Mrs. White, but I've hated you since the day you came to the café."

"You had every reason to hate me then. You were about to pop from the pregnancy, working your ass off every day at the cafe, and all we were worried about was how you would try to get money from Randy's estate. I am sorry for the mistakes I made, and I have paid dearly for them. Randy was our only child. We realized a long time ago that you were being truthful."

"Truthful? About what? I didn't go around town telling everyone I was pregnant with your son's child."

"Small town, Jenny. You know how things get around. There isn't a positive pregnancy test in this county that hasn't been heard about before the mother makes it home."

"I know. I've listened to all the bullshit for years at the café."

"I guess you heard that Earl Montgomery was hit by a freight train this afternoon?"

"No. I haven't seen anyone since I left work early and went home." Jenny didn't know Earl personally, although she'd seen him directing traffic for years. But the old man never came into the cafe to eat, at least not on her shift. She felt sick as she bent over her seat to ease the pain in her gut. "I guess we never know when our time will come."

"We suspected that Randy was the father of the girls. He'd told us about his date with you before he died."

Jenny looked at Mrs. White. "What did he say?" Her words were barely above a whisper.

"He said he'd had a wonderful time and was gonna bring you home to meet us."

"We never got to talk after our date. I never knew how he felt. He died before I knew I was pregnant. I never went out with anyone else."

"James, my husband, he always sees the worst in people. He thought you wanted money. He thought you slept around with people from the café."

"That son-of-a-bitch. I've had one date with Archie Snell since the girls were born. I've kissed one man in thirteen years."

"He knows that now, and I have made him miserable for it. I don't have much time left either. I have watched the girls grow up in this school, unable to hug them, or hold them, or even tell them how much I love them."

"That's enough," Jenny said. "I'll let you know what I decide. I will tell you personally."

"Do you have any idea how—?"

"I'll let you know before Thanksgiving. That will allow you to make plans for us if we decide to come for dinner."

"Thank you for listening to me."

Jenny got up and walked out the door.

***

After leaving the conference, Jenny stopped by the Wallace and Owens to pick up a loaf of bread and some milk. For the first time since she'd left the classroom, she could finally breathe. Her food stamps were left at home, but she'd made almost thirty dollars in tips that morning, and she never spent her food stamps in Delbert. Groceries weren't any cheaper at Success, however, she didn't have to look anyone in the eye and experience that condescending glance she had despised since her days at the Children's Home. Jenny never wanted anyone to feel sorry for her, and she had never wanted anyone to help her. Applying for food stamps had been the hardest thing to do, but Jenny knew the extra help made a huge difference in their lives.

The first application came in the mail after she'd called the Department of Human Services. Jenny always made it home an hour or so ahead of the twins, and the mail usually ran after the girls came home. Dana brought the envelope to her mother.

"What's this for?" Dana asked.

"I gotta fill this out and see if we live below the poverty line; they'll send us some extra money for groceries if we do," Jenny said.

"Can I help?" Donna asked. She'd come through the door just behind Dana.

"Get the calculator out of that drawer," Jenny said.

Donna retrieved the calculator and they sat at the table together as Jenny tried to recall and list all the money she'd made from her tips. Then she stood and pulled the utility bills from the wooden mail-holder that hung on the wall next to the refrigerator. Flipping through the bills, Jenny noted the monthly amounts for Southwestern Bell, Arkla Gas, and Craighead Electric. They didn't have a cable bill. Cable was a luxury they just couldn't afford. She almost forgot the water bill. She'd paid that a day ago and still had the receipt in her purse.

"Well, girls. It's official. We are below the poverty line," Jenny said.

Donna whooped and hollered, and Dana hooked her fingers inside her mouth and whistled.

"Can we get some good cereal now? And some chocolate milk?" Dana said.

Donna elbowed her sister. "I want some chocolate covered raisins and some of that Jimmy Dean Sausage Mr. Campbell serves at the café. Or some chocolate covered cherries."

"We'll all go to the store together and get whatever you want when they come in. But we need to try to make them last. They only come once a month. And we should buy some earthquake supplies, too. If that earthquake doesn't happen when predicted, it could still happen a day or a week later. We need to be prepared—"

"They cancelled school that day," Donna said. "Did you get the note?"

"Can we get cable with them?" Dana asked.

"No, and we can't buy tampons with them either." The girls giggled along with their mother. "I did get the note, though about school being cancelled for the earthquake. We'll spend that day making some of Ms. Grace's home-made fudge."

"Can we get some new shoes?"

"We can buy food, and that's it. After the first month, we'll see if we can save enough money to get cable. Now git. I gotta fix supper." The girls jumped from the table and headed for the door when Jenny stopped them.

"Listen. You don't need to tell anyone about this at school. Someone might make fun of you," Jenny said.

"They know better, Momma. We're twins," said Dana. She wrapped her arm around her sister, and they slid sideways through the screen door.

Jenny smiled. Life as a twin guaranteed at least one back-up in a scrap.

That started a monthly ritual. Since Jenny worked as a waitress and received tips for her wages, she had to complete a worksheet each month to qualify for assistance. At the end of each month, she and the girls sat and figured their income and expenses and toasted their poverty with a trip to the grocery store at Success where they stocked up on food and bought ice cream, or candy, or whatever treat they had craved for the past month.

The conference with Mrs. White had reminded Jenny that poverty was no laughing matter. She needed a better job. As Jenny walked through the aisles of the Wallace and Owens and looked at the items she couldn't afford or that she refused to buy until her food stamps came in, she thought of how helpless she'd be if the Whites suddenly decided to seek custody of the children.

At work every day customers talked of how a man couldn't win a custody battle, of how the courts almost never took a child away from its mother. But Jenny had seen many children removed from their parents and placed in the Children's Home. As one of the older children, Jenny became a big sister to the others who lived there. Every six months the cases of the children came before the Juvenile Court where Bill White, Randy White's father, represented the Children's Home in seeking continued custody of the children placed there by the state. Most of them came back from their court dates, but occasionally parents appeared in court with attorneys and took their children home. Jenny never got to say good-by.

She'd attended court more than once and watched the parents show up and tell the judge why their child should be allowed to come home. The ones with attorneys almost always won. Jenny didn't know how much an attorney cost, but she knew she couldn't afford one. Of course, she could always fuck Glen, her boss at the café. Her boss had always promised he'd give her anything if she would. And Jenny would do anything to keep her girls.

Jenny knew never to mistake sex for love. Jenny's mother, who couldn't stand the way her latest lover looked at her daughter, gave Jenny to the Department of Human Services, where Jenny celebrated her twelfth birthday as a ward of the State of Arkansas. Jenny never felt love until she had the twins, but sex was available at every foster home. Sometimes the advances came from an older sibling in the home, or from a neighbor, or relative. Twice the advances came from the head of the family that sheltered her. She knew not to complain about what happened. Complaints only caused problems, with the accusations always falling on her. Sex was the price she paid to live with her foster families. Jenny discovered she could survive by allowing the men or boys to do with her what they wanted.

She would not allow her daughters to experience that kind of life.

The advances came from the father at her last foster home. Steve Finnegan had started by coming into her room at night and masturbating as he lay on the floor next to her bed. That went on for weeks before he finally stood over the bed and ejaculated on her while he thought she lay sleeping. The night his wife caught him, they transferred Jenny to the Children's Home in Delbert. That was Jenny's fifteenth birthday.

Jenny walked past the Wonder Bread and the French rolls to the end of the aisle where the Best Choice loaves were signed "3 For a Dollar." She picked up a loaf and looked at the package. The plain bread sacks did not have an expiration date stamped on them. She put the bread back on the shelf. Backing up the aisle, she stopped in front of the Wonder Bread. The expiration date read "Nov.3rd" in bright red letters. The sign tagged on the shelf read "$1.00." Jenny grabbed two of the loaves and placed them in the child's seat of her cart. After walking down the aisle of earthquake supplies where she picked up a case of bottled water for her home reserves, she walked to the dairy section, bought a gallon of chocolate milk, and went home.

***

November fifth of 1990 was Election Day. Jenny worked her shift at the café and came home. As she waited for the girls to walk home from school, she thought of Thanksgiving. Her food stamps would come in the mail later in the week, and she'd use them to buy a turkey and all the trimmings for the traditional feast. As she kept looking down her grocery list, she knew she had forgotten something. Mandarin oranges.

The girls came in like a rush of wind through the door, laughing and giggling. They never seemed to fight, or even argue. Jenny never had a sister. The kids at the Children's Home had always seemed to be fighting—but not Donna and Dana.

"You two get in here and get something to eat. We gotta get down to the firehouse so I can vote."

"Do we have to go, Momma?" asked Dana.

"You need to see how simple it is," Jenny said.

"Why don't we ever have anyone over for the holidays? Sarah always goes to her grandmother's for Thanksgiving and Christmas. Don't we have any relatives?" Dana sat at the table with her mother, while Donna went to her room.

"Did Mrs. White say something to you about this?"

"No," Dana said.

"We have some relatives, somewhere. But we have each other. We don't need anyone else," Jenny said.

"Sarah wants us to go to her grandmother's for Thanksgiving. We wanna go," Dana said.

"You just gonna leave me alone? Besides, we have some place to go for Thanksgiving." Donna walked back into the kitchen and sat at the table.

"I don't wanna go to no employee dinner at the café. Mr. Campbell's dressing sucks," Dana stated.

"Watch your mouth, young lady. We have relatives to go see this Thanksgiving," said Jenny.

"You're too embarrassed to go around any of our relatives. Mooney Jr. told everyone at school we were on welfare and that you were a whore and didn't even know who our daddy was." Donna's eyes glistened.

Jenny got up and walked over to the filing cabinet. With her keys, she unlocked and opened the top drawer and reached inside. She tossed her daughter a box of Kleenex. "There," she said. Then she leaned over the file and continued her search. Donna blew her nose and wiped her eyes as her mother slammed the drawer and came back to the table. Jenny tossed the Voodoo book onto the table in front of them.

"When you go to school tomorrow, you cast a spell on that black bastard that'll shrivel his pecker," Jenny said.

"Momma."

"Listen to me." Jenny reached and clasped a hand of each of her girls. "His mother is white, and the preacher is white. He is black. That means the reverend cannot be his daddy. So he has no room to talk. If that fat little…boy says anything else about us, you go tell Mrs. White. In fact, you go tell her what he said when you go to school tomorrow."

"She's not our teacher anymore. We got a new one today."

"She has cancer," Donna added. "I'm gonna miss her, too. She always uses our papers as the best papers in the class."

Now Jenny understood.

"Let's get in the car and go vote," Jenny said.

"If the damned thing will start." Jenny didn't know which girl had muttered the words, and she didn't care. The old Monte Carlo might not start after all.

They pulled into the Delbert fire station just as the sun added mauve and orange hues to the horizon. The Union Pacific tracks created a meridian through the town, a de-facto demarcation from pole to pole between the haves and have-nots. A large crowd milled around in front of the station that served the wealthy side of the town. Sheriff Wilson Underwood and Buck Donnick, his opponent in the election, both stood on the sidewalks, shaking hands and soliciting votes for the last time. As Jenny and the girls walked up to the firehouse, a white truck with "Jester County Animal Control" painted on the door pulled up to the curb and parked in front of a fire hydrant. Jenny ran her arms through the arms of the twins and hurried off down the sidewalk.

"Jenny," Steve Finnegan said. He jumped out of the truck and ran after them. She acted like she didn't hear his words.

"Jenny," he shouted again as he tried to catch up.

"Someone is yelling at you, Momma," said Dana as she planted her feet and looked back over her shoulder.

"I didn't think you were gonna stop," Steve said as he finally caught up with them. He panted like he was out of breath.

"You'd think running with the dogs would keep an old cur like you in shape," Jenny said.

"So these are the twins I've heard so much about. You two are even prettier than your mother."

Jenny stepped forward, so close to Steve that their noses touched.

"If you ever speak to either of these girls, I'll kill you." She spoke in a low voice with a deliberate pace as she emphasized each syllable of every word. "I'll cut off that dick that you are so fond of playing with and I'll stuff it in your mouth. When they find you, you'll look like one of those armadillos you're always propping up on the road with a beer bottle in its paws." Jenny turned and started walking on up the sidewalk. Donna and Dana stood looking first at the man who had provoked such a reaction from their mother, then at Jenny's back as she walked away. They trotted after her.

"I only did one armadillo, Jenny. Someone else is doing them now. I just wanted to say hi. I haven't seen you since you left the house," he said as he followed the girls up the sidewalk. "That's been nearly fifteen years or so. Marilyn and I are divorced now."

Jenny spun around and touched noses with the man again.

"If I even see that white truck in my neighborhood after school lets out, I'll kill you, Steve."

"That's big talk for a bitch like you. You might wake up dead, yourself," he said.

"All those nights I lay in that bed pretending nothing was happening. I don't play pretend anymore."

"I just thought we might go out sometime," he said.

Jenny laughed and turned to continue up the sidewalk. The twins stepped immediately to her side. They linked their arms through the arms of their mother and carried her, as Jenny nearly collapsed.

"Momma, are you ok? What was that about?" Dana asked.

"We'll put a spell on that bastard, too. Same one we put on Mooney Junior," Donna said.

Jenny smiled. Apparently, being the mother of twins guaranteed two backups in a scrap. They got their red hair from their father. No one, not even Mrs. White, could deny that. But the fire in those green eyes belonged to Jenny. They'd learned the bad language while sitting in a booth at the café, waiting for Jenny to finish her shifts. Treating the girls as equals, whenever she could, had always been Jenny's way. She scolded them for their language at times, but their lives were not simple. She didn't expect the girls to talk like Harvard lawyers. Jenny never wanted the girls to know or experience what had happened to her. Someday, when they were older, she might tell them. She taught her girls early about sex, explained the difference between a good touch and a bad touch, told them that adults did not keep secrets with children, and that they would never be punished for telling her if someone touched them in the wrong way.

Steve Finnegan, however, still wore a badge—even if he was just the dogcatcher.

After she placed her vote, Jenny took the girls home. Finnegan was nowhere around as they left the building. They sat up late that night, popped popcorn, and watched a movie they'd rented at the video rental in the Wallace and Owens store. The next morning was still a school day. That night, it didn't matter. Jenny didn't want to be alone, never again. After dialing Archie Snell's number, she got a recording. She left a message.

"Hi. This is Jenny. I just wondered if we're ever gonna see each other again. Not in the café. Call me," she said.

She didn't understand how a person could live with thirty other kids like she had at the Children's Home and feel so alone. As she sat on the couch and laughed with her girls, she remembered how her life had been before Donna and Dana. She'd had no life. Her own mother's face appeared as a blur in her memory, surrounded by dark hair that fell over ample breasts. Doreen. At least she could remember her name. Doreen had called from Las Vegas after the twins were born. She'd called the Children's Home, and they gave her the number at Campbell's. Glen, after being told Doreen was Jenny's mother, told her Jenny was at the hospital with twin girls. When he answered no, Jenny hadn't married, Doreen hung up and never called again.

Jenny knew her life had been different because of her mother. The twins' lives were different because of her. But Jenny had no one. If Steve Finnegan ever made good on his threat to kill her, or if she ever had an accident like Earl Montgomery, the girls would go to foster care, or to the same home she had. What if that earthquake really happened? Acknowledging the Whites as the girl's grandparents would, at least, give them someone to care for them. It would also give them someone who could easily take them away.

If Mrs. White were to die of cancer, the girls would be devastated. But couldn't the love of a grandmother, even for a short time, compensate for the pain of such a devastating loss? Having never experienced such love, Jenny couldn't answer her own question.

A vehicle eased past the house; its lights crawling across the living room walls. Jenny refused to go to the window to look out. If it was Finnegan, he would want her to be looking for him.

She picked up the phone and left another message on Archie's answering machine.

***

Jenny took her turkey out of the refrigerator early Thanksgiving morning. She stirred meal and eggs into a bowl to make cornbread for dressing. Donna and Dana had been quiet the past week, and they had repeatedly asked if they could go to Sarah's to eat. Jenny repeatedly told them no.

With butter she'd bought at Success with her food stamps, she prepared the turkey for the oven. She left big, yellow lumps under the skin of the breast. Then she slipped her fingers under the skin of the thigh and leg and left more. The butter would melt and baste the meat as the turkey baked, keeping the bird from drying out. Miss Grace, the cook at the Children's Home, had shown her the trick one holiday morning when Jenny woke hours before the other children and couldn't go back to sleep.

The staff and faculty at the orphanage tried their best to create a family atmosphere. When Jenny thought about her days at the home, she realized just how hard the staff had tried. No matter what they had done, the holidays always seemed lonely.

Many times Jenny woke up early and went to the kitchen where Miss Grace let her help with the holiday meal. Sometimes the old cook would give Jenny an open can of Mandarin oranges, a special treat Miss Grace kept hidden away in the cabinets for the times Jenny would come to see her.

"Why aren't you home with your family today?" Jenny asked her one Christmas.

Miss Grace continued to cut biscuits from the dough she had rolled out on the table in front of her. Holiday mornings kept her busy as she prepared breakfast and dinner meals at the same time. Grace looked to be about sixty years old, although she never told anyone her real age. "The day I retire will be the day they place me six feet under," she always said. As broad as she was tall, she looked like a stump. She reminded Jennie of a white version of Mammie, from *Gone With the Wind,* the way she fussed after the children. Dressed in gray slacks, a blue flannel shirt with the sleeves rolled up to her elbows, a white apron, and a hairnet, Miss Grace always had a special treat for any of the children who wandered into her kitchen. Jenny never had a grandmother, but she always wanted one like Miss Grace. "My daughters cook supper for me the day before Christmas," she said. "That way I can take care of you children. You need me more than they do."

Jenny walked to the phone and picked up the directory. She dialed the Whites' home number. Mrs. White answered the phone.

"I have a turkey and some dressing that I'm just now putting in the oven. We could be there about eleven. Do you need me to get anything from the store before we come over?"

"Could you get some cranberry sauce, Jenny? Get some jellied and whole berry if you don't mind. And a bag of ice," Mrs. White said. "The Wallace and Owens is open today. I'll pay you for it when you get here."

"I got cranberry sauce, both kinds. I can get the ice," Jenny said. The phone went silent for just a few moments before Jenny spoke again. "I'll tell the girls before we come over today."

"We'll be ready for you when you get here." Mrs. White could not hide the excitement in her voice.

"Why didn't you tell me about the cancer?

"Would it have made any difference?" Mrs. White asked.

"No. Not to me. Not then."

After she placed the phone back on the receiver, Jenny put the turkey in the oven. She wiped down the table and opened a can of Mandarin oranges. She dumped the contents in a Tupperware bowl and tossed the empty can in the trash. Then she walked down the hall to wake her sleeping daughters.

The Mayor of Delbert, Arkansas

After he thumped the microphone in front of him three times, Chuck Powell, Mayor of Delbert, Arkansas, and manager of Delbert's only grocery store – called the city council meeting to order.

"Can I have your attention please? If everyone will be seated, we'll get things started." After most of the crowd had been seated, Chuck spoke again.

"We don't have enough copies for everyone, but an *Earthquake Survival Guide*, published by the Red Cross, is being passed around. As you all know, Iben Browning has predicted the exact date of our next earthquake here on the New Madrid Fault. I guess normally this wouldn't be such a big deal, but he did get it right when he predicted that last earthquake in San Francisco. So whether he gets it right again this time, and we hope he's wrong of course, his prediction has brought attention to how unprepared we are for such a catastrophe."

"I got somethin' I wanna say about this beer permit." Zeluka Biggs stood in the middle of the courtroom. She wore a yellow dress covered with huge sunflowers. If Zeluka herself hadn't been so large, there wouldn't have been but a couple of blooms on the dress. Nearly as large as Zeluka, the purse that hung from her arm could have held a case of beer and still had room for all her things. Zeluka's voice was as big as she was.

"Hello, Zeluka," Chuck said. "I promise you'll get your chance, but I need to cover a few preliminary things to set tonight's agenda first." After ten years of service and four re-elections to two-year terms, Chuck still loved listening to the banter of politics. At the local level, people defined their issues narrowly. They saw agendas in simple terms: how much will this cost me tomorrow, and is it a sin.

"We don't need any more beer joints in this county, Mayor Powell. If we let another beer joint in here, we'll have crack houses and whore houses and casinos on every street before we know it."

"Zeluka, I'll give you a chance here in just a minute. I'm almost through. Please let me finish covering the agenda, and I'll let

79

you go first, even though I already promised to let someone else begin the discussion."

"I got more I wanna say about this," Zeluka said as she sat back down.

"Anyway, we have a lot to do to make sure our community is prepared. Just because the earthquake is predicted to hit on December 2nd doesn't mean it couldn't come earlier, or any day thereafter. The city has applied, and been approved, for a grant to educate the public and buy emergency equipment to better prepare for an earthquake, or any other natural catastrophe, like a tornado. I'm sure most of you remember the tornadoes that hit Jonesboro back a few years ago. I wasn't expecting this big a crowd tonight, or I'd have had more copies of the guide ordered. I'll get more copies and leave them at City Hall and down at the store for anyone interested in picking them up."

"We also have earthquake supplies set aside in the store where items like bottled water, Spam, Vienna Sausages, batteries and first aid kits are all marked down to cost.

"We have Wink Gaskill's retail beer permit for public discussion tonight. We'll discuss the application first, since the Reverend Marrs' church is here, represented by Attorney Tuffy Howard, who has asked to address this meeting. Everyone here needs to know that if the City Council takes no action, this permit will be approved. To have any effect on the permit application, a motion objecting to the permit must be made, seconded by a council member, and then passed by a majority vote. If no resolution is passed, the permit will be approved by the State Alcohol Beverage Commission. Now, with the Council's permission, I'd like to recognize Attorney Tuffy Howard."

Zeluka Biggs shot up from her seat. "You said I could go first, Chuck."

A ripple of laughter flowed across the room.

"Mayor, please allow Ms. Biggs to proceed. I have no problems yielding the floor," Tuffy said. Reverend Mooney Marrs groaned and shifted in his seat. Every minute cost Marrs more money. He'd asked for a special offering to combat this permit last Sunday at church and even placed the event on the church prayer bulletin, along with all of the other decrepit sinners in the community. Any money that didn't go to the attorney would go in the preacher's pocket.

Zeluka didn't wait for the Mayor to acknowledge her.

"I've lived here all of my life, and I like Wink Gaskill. He seems to be a good man, except for the fact he sells booze for a living. I don't know how he got to be a member of Mooney Marrs' church. Now Marrs is here with an attorney fighting one of his own deacons. That could never have happened at a Pentecostal church."

"That's because he tithes about fifty thousand a year to Mooney's church, Zeluka," said Posey Eubanks from where he sat in the back of the courtroom.

"Half of the problems in this county are caused by boozing and womanizing," Zeluka said. "Wink Gaskill gets called to testify in every divorce case in this county. Ain't but one reason, and that's all our men go up there to chase them floozies he has working for him."

Chuck Powell waited patiently for Zeluka's tirade to end, but finally gave up and interrupted. "Zeluka, we ain't here to crucify Wink or his employees. This is a hearing about the permit application. We need to keep our comments to what you perceive to be the good or bad effects that approval of this permit will have on the community."

"That's what I said earlier. We'll have crack houses and whore houses and casinos on every street corner if we let them set up another beer joint."

Glen Campbell, the owner of Campbell's Café and the council representative from Ward Three spoke. "He isn't applying for a beer joint, Zeluka. He's applied for a permit to sell beer at a convenience store he wants to build out east of town. No one can drink beer on those premises," Glen said.

"Well, if they can't get drunk there, you know what'll happen," Zeluka said. Her hair had fallen down, and she jerked her head as she spoke. Chuck remembered how worked up she used to get when she testified at Mooney Marrs' church, before they ran her off for being too loud. "They'll just drink it on the way home, and we'll have more DWI's and people dying on our highways."

"Well, Zeluka's got one thing right," said Larry Liddell from the front row. A small man in his late fifties, Larry could drink a case of beer before breakfast—and usually did. "I got two DWI's last year driving over to Success to get my beer. If I could drive into Delbert and buy it, I wouldn't have to be on the road so long. I could be home in fifteen minutes and wouldn't have to be hassled by Sheriff Underwood or any of his *Barney Fife* deputies. You can't buy any carry out at Wink's bar, and they's no other place that sells beer in town since the state shut down Harvey Knuckles for not paying his sales tax."

T.E. Trantham stood up. "Drinking is a sin and should not be allowed in this town. We can't do anything about Wink's place, but we can keep any more beer joints from coming in."

From over in the east corner of the building came Buddy Jones' booming voice. "That's the problem with you damned Holy Rollers. You want to legislate morality for everyone. You idiots don't understand that freedom of religion means you can serve God any way you want. But you don't have to serve if you don't want to. Calling this a sin is like saying Jesus sinned when he turned the water into wine—"

"Jesus did not turn the water into wine," Reverend Mooney Marrs said from where he sat, squirming. "Wine was the collective term for the fruit of the vine."

"Preacher, that's one of the oldest lies you folks tell," Buddy said. "Wine is wine throughout the ages. They couldn't keep fresh juice back then, so they fermented it. Or rather they let it ferment. They couldn't keep from it, unless they threw it out. I saw it on the History Channel just the other day." Buddy Jones paused for a second—just long enough to reach up, remove his hat, and run his fingers through his white hair. "I done forgot what I was saying now. But that History Channel does have some good shows on it." The old man sat back down.

Chuck saw his chance to take control of the discussion. "Attorney Howard, would you like to address this meeting?"

Tuffy Howard's name was well known around Delbert. Tales of the million dollar cases Tuffy had tried and settled were told and retold. Even Tuffy laughed at the status of his reputation. "If I'd won as many million dollar cases as they said I have, I'd have more money than Sam Walton."

But Tuffy knew how to make a point. He could reach down to the level of his audience. His presence and demeanor expanded and filled any room he entered: like air expanding a balloon. Although Tuffy could wear the most expensive suits made—and he did wear them when he argued before the Arkansas Supreme Court—he wore cheap blazers and wrinkled trousers whenever he appeared anywhere else for his clients. He believed a common man on a jury could not relate to an attorney wearing a suit that cost half a year's salary for a working man. As Tuffy stood up from his seat, the room became silent. He looked disheveled and wrinkled. The arms of his jacket were too short, and his tie came to the indentation of his navel in the white shirt he wore. Under his pot belly, his loose slacks hung precariously, secured by a black leather belt and red suspenders that flashed when his jacket flew open. His reading glasses hung down on the end of his nose so he could look over them. He couldn't read with them anyway; Tuffy wore them because he thought they made him look scholarly.

"Mayor Powell, City Councilmen, citizens of Delbert, and Ms. Zeluka Biggs," said Tuffy as he bowed slightly in the direction of Ms. Biggs. "Thank you for giving me an opportunity to address this meeting tonight on behalf of the congregation of Reverend Mooney Marrs' church. The Reverend Marrs and his parishioners are concerned, deeply concerned, about this retail beer permit and the effects it will have on the Delbert community. They have asked me to present these concerns to the council."

Tuffy moved from the front row of seats and slid the podium off to the side of the room so he could look at the council and the audience at the same time. The squeaking of the podium castors and the swooshing of the ceiling fans seemed loud.

"Wink Gaskill has applied for a retail beer permit. This will allow him to sell carry-out booze at the convenience store he is building out east of town. I am holding an affidavit signed by 132 members of Mooney Marrs' church. This document represents the wishes of 132 citizens of Delbert who do not want another beer joint in their community."

Chuck said, "Can I see that document, Mr. Howard?"

"Certainly." Tuffy left the podium and strode forward to present the affidavit to the mayor. Tuffy then returned to the podium where he waited to make sure he had the mayor's attention before he continued. After giving the paper a cursory glance, Mayor Powell passed it to Boo-Boo James, the city councilman sitting to his right. Chuck noticed the silence. He looked up at the attorney and nodded. Tuffy continued.

"Booze kills a community. Look at Halliday. After they opened that beer store out there, that was it. The community was stunted."

Lydia Friar, the councilwoman who sat at the end of the table to Chuck Powell's right, now held the church affidavit in her hands. Everyone in the room, except Tuffy Howard, knew she was Wink Gaskill's niece. She interrupted the attorney.

"Are you trying to say that Halliday has not grown because it has a liquor store?"

"Exactly. If you—"

"Now, Tuffy, Halliday is a bend in the road on the way to Marmaduke. That bend got its name when Riley Jones put that liquor store out there. That place wouldn't even have a name if it wasn't for that store."

"I am sorry, ma'am, but I don't know your name, so I am not sure how to address you," Tuffy said.

"I am Councilwoman Lydia Friar."

"Well now, Lydia, the history of—"

"No, sir. You misunderstood me. I am Councilwoman Lydia Friar."

Tuffy spoke again. "The history of Halliday—"

"Attorney Howard, getting this council to pass a resolution for your clients will be impossible if you piss me off, and I move to stop your speech."

"I'll second any motion you make, Councilwoman Lydia Friar," Boo-Boo James said.

"Forgive me, Councilwoman Lydia Friar. In my haste to make my point as quickly as I could, I have forgotten all courtesies. Please, do not hold my ignorance against my clients."

"You still have the floor, sir. You may continue; but first I have a question. What does the store at Halliday have to do with this retail beer permit application?"

"Halliday had everything needed to become a metropolis; a major highway, railroad lines, good soil. Now it's a bend in the road named for a beer store."

"I remember a Union Pacific track goes through Halliday. Mike Thompson was killed there years ago," said Councilwoman Lydia Friar. "But just because trains come zipping through there at seventy miles an hour doesn't mean they have access to a rail line."

"Councilwoman Lydia Friar, the railroad will install a spur line anywhere if industry needs it."

"And are you calling Highway One a good highway, Mr. Howard?"

"It is a major highway. Yes. I am saying that."

"That road is called Highway One because it was the first paved highway in the state of Arkansas. I don't think it's been resurfaced since."

Boo-Boo James said, "I think you're right about that, Councilwoman Lydia Friar." Wink Gaskill was his stepfather.

Laughter stirred through the warm courtroom where the bodies of the overflowing crowd were pressed together. The room temperature had elevated to a point that made the audience become restless—removing coats and using the Red Cross Earthquake Survival Guides for fans. The men who leaned against the back wall of the courtroom shifted their weight from one leg to another, but never in rhythm, their movements keeping time like popcorn in a microwave.

"Councilwoman Lydia Friar, if we allow this store to come in, we'll have more DWI's, more crime. Any new tax revenues from the extra sales of booze would undoubtedly be offset by the devastation to the city. Jobs lost because of alcoholism, marriages ruined—"

"All those DWI's would help some," Devon Garrett said from the back of the room. "When I got mine over at Success, they fined me over two thousand dollars. If I gotta pay a fine, I'd rather keep that money here in Delbert."

"I expected this issue to come up," Chuck said. "So I asked the City Attorney, Randy Johnson, to do some research on DWI's in Jester County, and in Success. Randy, what did you find out?"

"Well, over in Greene County, to the south of us, they had fifty one DWI's. But they also have twice the population of Jester County. So does Clay County to the east. So I adjusted the DWI figures to per capita, meaning the DWI's adjusted to reflect how many people live in the area, and Jester County had twice as many DWI's per capita as any other county around us."

Tuffy Howard spoke immediately. "See there. This county already leads the region in DWI's. Another beer joint can only exacerbate that problem."

"Well, now that's not exactly right, Tuffy," Randy Johnson said. "This is a wet county, but we don't have any places that sell carry-out beer in Delbert. All we have is Wink's Night Club out on the by-pass, and you have to buy a membership there and drink inside. Seems most of our DWI's are local residents going to buy beer in a neighboring county and getting arrested on the way home."

"That's how I got mine," Devon Garrett said.

Jim Billy Griffin stood up across the room from Devon Garrett. "I never got no DWI's. But I wear out a new truck ever' three years just driving over to Success to buy beer. It'd be nice to buy it here in town again, even if it was more expensive."

As he watched the debate, Chuck wondered how it would feel to sit in the state legislature. Many of his friends called him "Governor," but Chuck had no aspirations for state political office. At the local level, even one person could make a difference. A tax issue to fund a new gymnasium for the Delbert Community Center had passed by three votes. Five senior citizens had called him and complained that the youth in Delbert had no place to go. The kids needed that gym. But they couldn't drive to the polls to vote. Chuck had arranged transportation for all of them. After that election, Chuck had gone to their houses and explained how they could get an absentee ballot. The ballots would be mailed to them before the next elections took place.

Politics at the state and national levels had lost sight of the little man. Since he began working as a clerk at the grocery store,

Chuck had always seen his role as one of service to his customers and his community. Finding a can of chili, coaching a girls' softball team because no one else would volunteer, giving the local youth a chance for a job before they left for college, helping to pass a tax issue that would provide better services to the citizens of Delbert—Chuck strived to have an impact on the lives of those around him, no matter how menial the task seemed.

Being involved at the state level might give him the ability to do more. When his fiancée, Sally Brewer, was diagnosed with acute paranoid schizophrenia, he had worked with Sally's parents to try to help her. But at every level it seemed that mental disease carried the stigma that AIDS had carried in the early eighties. There was no funding for care or assistance for people afflicted with the disease. Private insurance carriers refused to pay for treatment.

***

After he broke off his engagement to Sally, she came to the store to see him. She had cleaned herself up and fixed her hair, but Chuck could see the fresh lines where she'd cut her arms with a razor before coming to the store. She asked to speak to him in private. They walked into his office, and he closed the door.

"Chuck, if I take my medicine, I can be like anyone else. I still love you, and I need you," Sally said.

Chuck sat in his chair and found it hard to look into Sally's eyes. But he did.

"I can't deal with this, Sally. You've already been cutting yourself again this morning," he said.

"I did that when I fell with a glass."

"I don't believe you," Chuck said.

"Fine." She got up and walked to the door. Then she stopped and turned to him one last time. "If I'd had cancer, I know you'd have stood beside me. If I were sick from chemo, you'd be there holding the bucket I puked in. I know you love me. Why is this different?"

At first, Chuck didn't know what to say. He searched for an answer, one that might be comforting to her. He could think of none. So he spoke the truth that came to him.

"If you had cancer, Sally, you'd either die or recover. You will never be free of this, and I can't watch you suffer."

"I guess I can live with that. Too bad I didn't get cancer, huh?" Sally walked out the door.

***

Tuffy Howard had allowed the audience to take over the conversation. His gravelly voice now boomed over the unorganized banter, and the room fell silent as he spoke.

"On behalf of all of the citizens of Delbert represented by that affidavit, and the hundreds of people who support our position but were unable to sign the document, I ask this council to pass a resolution specifically condemning this permit application and expressing the will of the citizens of Delbert that we have no more beer joints in this county."

"Thank you, Tuffy," Chuck Powell said. "Now I want to open the floor for comments from the public."

"It's about time," said Zeluka Biggs as she jumped back to her feet. "If you let this beer joint in here, we'll have crack houses, whore houses, and casinos on every street corner in Delbert. I don't want to live in no Babylon."

From somewhere in the crowd, someone shouted "Amen, sister."

"Now, Ms. Biggs," Macon Huckaby said. He sat on the left of Chuck Powell, next to Randy Johnson. A city council member for over twenty years, Macon owned the Sears Appliance Store out on the bypass next to Wink's Nightclub. "Aren't you buying a house over in Success? I believe I heard this morning at Campbell's Café that you were closing on it next week?"

"You darned right I am. I heard about this beer permit and decided it was time to leave," Zeluka Biggs said.

"But the last time I counted, Ms. Biggs, Success had ten bars, three night clubs, and fifteen places where a person can buy carry-out beer. Were you able to find a neighborhood without any crack houses, whorehouses, or casinos, or did you plan to open one of your own?"

"Macon Huckaby, you calling me a whore?" Zeluka, who had been sitting in the middle of a row of seats five rows back, now stumbled over the people to her left as she struggled to make it to the aisle. She bristled like a game rooster with new steel strapped to his legs. "I'll climb across that table and kick your sorry ass."

Sheriff Wilson Underwood stepped forward to the edge of the council table. Chuck Powell had watched Wilson move like that before. Many times, just the visible presence of a uniform had a calming effect. Jack Ditta, the Delbert City Marshall, stood at the other end of the table. Chuck wondered if Zeluka Biggs, a large but agile woman, could jump the council table. He had no doubts she could have whipped Macon Huckaby if she ever got her hands on him.

"No, Ms. Biggs. I'm not saying anything of the sort. Please, sit back down. It just seems ridiculous for you to come before this council talking the way you are about this permit application, when you're moving to a home just around the corner from a tavern."

Tuffy Howard jumped to his feet. "What the lady is trying to say is that she can do nothing about the established joints, but she can be heard about setting up a new one."

"Mr. Howard," said Councilwoman Lydia Friar. "You've had your chance to address this council. Be seated." Tuffy Howard eased back into his chair. "What's being exposed here is the hypocritical nature of this woman's complaint. She won't even be living in Delbert, whether this permit is approved or not."

"We need another store," Maydeane Gossett said. She taught Kindergarten at the Delbert Elementary School. "It will create more jobs and competition, and no one can deny that extra tax revenue is needed. But does Wink have to sell beer, to be able to make the store work?"

Andy Hartsoe stood and spoke next. "The question is one of return on equity. I studied that during my two years of business school at the university. These stores are expensive to build and operate. The one over at Marmaduke closed and reopened four times in the past six years. They can't sell beer. If Wink is gonna build this thing, he needs to be able to make as much money as he can. That's why he needs the beer permit. Now, those of you who say you want the store, but don't

89

want the beer sold there, why don't you go down to the Delbert Bank with Wink and just sign on his note with him? See if you want the permit denied then."

The political debate had turned to personal taunts, and Chuck knew it was time to move on. Sin issues could never be resolved. There could never be a compromise with religious fundamentalists, so he interrupted the debate.

"I believe this has gone on long enough. We have more important issues to discuss tonight. So if any member of this council has any motion to make with regard to Wink Gaskill's beer permit, so move."

For the first time since the meeting had started, the room fell silent. Chuck looked around the courtroom, waiting for someone at the council table to make a motion. Then the side door opened and Sally Brewer walked in.

Sally wore a pair of old jeans so tight she couldn't snap or zip them. A crimson stain marked the crotch of her pants. Chuck knew from his discussions with Darlene, Sally's mother, that Sally's period made her sickness worse. A filthy tee-shirt barely covered her abdomen, and Chuck could see the red stripes across her stomach where Sally had carved on herself again.

"With no motions made by the council, this debate is closed." Chuck said.

"I have a motion," Sally said. "I just came from the doctor's office. He said I'm not schizo anymore. Said he made a big mistake. Said I have leukemia, and that I should die from it soon." As she spoke, she walked to the council table and stood in front of Chuck. "Can we get married now?"

Chuck heard the laughter and snickers in the courtroom. The Mayor of Delbert, Arkansas, jumped to his feet and shouted, "Shut the fuck up."

The room fell silent.

Sheriff Wilson Underwood stepped around the end of the table, again.

Glen Campbell said, "I move we recess for fifteen minutes then return and discuss our earthquake preparations."

Boo-Boo James seconded the motion and called a vote; the council passed it unanimously.

As everyone sat still, Chuck extended his hand to Sally. "Come with me, Sally," he said.

"Can we go to the courthouse and get our marriage license now?"

"We need to stop by the hospital first and have you checked in," Chuck said. He walked around the table and up to Sally. He took her in his arms and hugged her.

"I'll go if you'll take me up there," she said.

He turned to the council members and said, "I'll be right back. Sheriff, can you walk us out to my car?"

Sheriff Wilson Underwood led Sally and Chuck out the side door.

Nearly an hour later, Chuck returned to the council meeting. When he entered the courtroom foyer, he saw a copy of the *Red Cross Earthquake Survival Guide* on the floor. Chuck picked it up and browsed through the table of contents as he considered which part was most important. All of the suggestions were vital, but securing the home so items wouldn't fall off the shelf during the quake, and setting aside an adequate supply of food and water would be the first items he covered. Before he could walk into the courtroom, he bumped into Tuffy Howard.

"Mayor Powell." Tuffy stood before him with his hand extended. Chuck accepted the attorney's vigorous handshake. "We've heard all the way over to Success about you marking down the earthquake supplies at your store. That's ingenious. You must be running for governor."

Chuck managed the Wallace and Owens grocery store in Delbert, and he'd stockpiled earthquake supplies. All those items were pulled out and marked down to cost. Two of his clerks hung an "Earthquake Supplies" banner at both ends of the aisle.

"I marked those down hoping people would buy them and get prepared for this thing. I have no plans to run for governor, or any other office. The store owners nearly fired me for it." Chuck grinned.

"You jest," Tuffy said.

"I may be the Mayor of Delbert, but I'm just another employee at Wallace and Owens," Chuck said.

"Firing the Mayor of the city for marking down vitally needed survival supplies wouldn't be good for business," Tuffy said. "How is the young lady?"

"She's off her medicine and menstruating. For her, it's a deadly combination," Chuck said.

"I've handled civil commitments for most of my career. There is no help for mental illness. Anywhere," Tuffy said.

"I'm sorry the council couldn't pass the resolution you wanted. I hope you were paid in advance."

"Always paid in advance," Tuffy said. Then he placed his hand on Chuck's shoulder. The old attorney had a way of appearing patriarchal without seeming condescending. "I was geared up to leave, but I think I'll stick around for your little hearing. See if I can learn something about how to prepare for this earthquake they say we're gonna have. You think ole Iben Browning will get it right again, the exact date of the earthquake?"

"Doesn't matter, Tuffy. It doesn't matter if it ever happens in our lifetime. But it could, and we gotta be ready."

"Kinda reminds me of the old fall-out shelters we used to keep supplied back during the Russian days," Tuffy said.

"Well, if I don't get this called to order, we'll be here all night." They walked through the doors of the courtroom.

"Sheriff Underwood, please tell everyone we're about to begin," Chuck said. "They need to come back in and take their seats."

Tuffy Howard returned to his chair, and the city council members sat back down at the council table. Chuck called the meeting to order. Then he looked around the empty room for Sheriff Underwood, who stood to his left.

"Wilson, is there anyone else left out there?" Chuck asked.

"No, sir, your honor. Everyone was here for the beer permit. Most of them left when you took Sally to the hospital. The others got tired of waiting."

After he looked around the empty room, Chuck got up and gathered the *Red Cross Earthquake Survival Guides* left in the chairs.

Some lay in the floor. The members of the city council waited in silence.

Chuck turned back to the council table. "Randy, you know what has to be done to qualify for the grant. You have a quorum. Take over for me."

The chilly October night greeted the mayor as he exited the building and walked to his Dodge truck. After he left the city square, he drove out into the county, out by Scatter Creek. There was a place there in the wildlife management area where Chuck used to take Sally for picnics, where they lay on the bank of the lake and made love and counted the falling stars. Then her behavior became erratic, and her sickness took control of her life, and their relationship.

He went there by himself now. The lake had been re-stocked with fish, and he could always count on a nice stringer of bream, when he had the time. Wild blackberry briars covered the backside of the levee. The honks of a small flock of Canadian geese broke his trance, and he saw silhouettes of the huge birds, illuminated by the brilliance of a million stars.

A governor keenly aware of the problems facing the mentally ill and the families who loved them could make a big difference. Chuck believed he could make a difference, but although he felt he could do the job, he knew he would never try for the office.

Tomorrow, he would mark down more of the supplies. After reading the survival guide, he knew more about what was needed. The people of his town might not be ready when the earthquake finally happened, but it wouldn't be his fault.

Karen

Karen loved her early morning shower. Standing inside the stone-lined stall she directed all four nozzles so that every inch of her body could feel the pulsing waves of the steaming water. If she placed one of the heads at a certain angle, she could feel the water striking the barbell of her vertical hood piercing. She hadn't removed the metal in the four years since being pierced at a tattoo parlor in Memphis, and Dan still had not noticed. Jenny had told her the piercing would increase her sensitivity during sex, but the only thing that had changed was her ability to climax in the shower every morning without Dan or her toys. The water was hot – not hot enough to burn, but hot enough to leave a pink glow to her skin when she toweled off. The body soap she used smelled of lavender and honeysuckle, and after applying half of the bottle to her washcloth she began to lather her body, gently rubbing over her stomach, down her legs, and across her shoulders. The fragrance would cling to her skin no matter how long her day. She added conditioner to her hair. Earlier in the week she'd seen her beautician for highlights to hide the gray now beginning to show. Her hair had betrayed her years ago – turning gray long before she was ready, but her body had done well; her breasts would be the envy of any eighteen-year-old girl. The laugh lines had disappeared during her years of marriage to Dr. Dan Crabtree. Crow's feet ringed her eyes. She remembered her reservations at the Peabody, and her appointment with the surgeon in Memphis next week. Her doctor had performed all of Priscilla Presley's work and claimed he could remove twenty years of age from around her eyes.

As hot water rinsed the conditioner from her hair, she remembered that Dan hadn't come to bed last night. Karen knew where she'd find him. She stepped out, toweling herself dry as she stole glimpses at the floor-length mirror. Finally she stopped, dropped the towel and stared. She'd added twenty pounds in the years since she married Dan, but most of it had gone to her breasts and hips, enhancing the curve of her body that Dan had seemed to love. She cupped her breasts and lifted them, then smiled at herself. Turning from the mirror, she walked to her make-up counter where she sat and lit a cigarette. She knew people who claimed that smoking after sex enhanced the effect, but for her, sitting to smoke a cigarette after standing in the shower for an orgasm never made sense. Half-way through the cigarette, she stubbed it out. Looking through the bottles of perfume, she found the Private Collection, back behind Dr. Dan's favorites. Dan never cared for anything by Estée Lauder, and his aversion had nothing to do with the fragrance.

She picked up the bottle of perfume and sprayed herself, inhaling the enveloping mist. Her naked body tingled as the perfume evaporated from her skin, and she remembered how Jake, on their first night together, had found her bottle and sprayed the bed with the fragrance. Their love making that night had been interrupted by the rising sun, when Jake stopped long enough to take the cocoa butter he warmed in the microwave and massaged her from head to toe, carefully rubbing and stroking her. As he worked his way down her body, he pressed the lotion into the back of her legs, his fingers rubbing her inner thighs, pressing the flesh against her bones, coming closer and closer with every powerful stroke until he gently brushed against her, once, then twice, then he moved down to massage her calves. He rubbed the lotion between each of her toes, along the soles of her feet, and on her ankles. She called him a tease. He laughed. She had stopped the massage to fill a more urgent need.

Her cheeks felt warm with the memory, and she was pleased to find her face could still turn to a crimson hue. She wondered if she blushed at the memory, or the chance she might see Jake tonight at Delbert.

She had dated Jake while still in nursing school. Jake even helped her study for her boards. She broke it off when he started working on the riverboats. Soon after, she met and married Dr. Dan Crabtree.

This morning was not just about old memories. Karen wanted to buy a storefront property in Delbert, Arkansas. Tired of the arrogance she experienced from anyone associated with the medical profession, she had decided to pursue her interest in fashion design. A fabric shop would allow her a space to work on her ideas and creations and a means to support her passion. She didn't need to make a profit from the venture so much as she needed something to occupy her time. She could no longer simply wait for Dan to drink himself to death. Attorney James White would meet her at Campbell's Café at 9:00.

After slipping into her robe she stepped out on her balcony. On one end sat the planters she'd bought with the new Boston ferns that would eventually replace the withered ones now hanging from the rails. She strolled back inside to the sink, filled her water pot and returned, leaning over the railing to water the old plants. A flock of wild turkeys grazed across the back yard, carefully selecting acorns and grasshoppers as they scratched through the mulch of fallen leaves. Their back yard was also home to a small herd of deer, and a couple of groundhogs. She wondered if Jake still hung out at Wink's, or if he'd be out on a riverboat. His uncle Freddie owned the Schugtown Farmer's Co-op, and she'd heard that Jake had taken over a large part of the operation. Freddie had bought a river-boat company and Jake ran tugs up and down the Mississippi and through the intra-coastal waterway all the way down to Brownsville, up the Arkansas to Tulsa, and up the Ohio past Cincinnati. While on the boats, Jake worked thirty days at a time, and then was home for thirty days. But Jenny told her just yesterday that Jake was off the boats and taking flying lessons, as his uncle was expanding further into crop-dusting services. It seemed Freddie was grooming Jake to take over the business. Jake occasionally pitched in and helped Wink Gaskill at Wink's Bar on weekends. Wink was another of Jake's uncles. It seemed that anytime she needed to bump into Jake she could go to Wink's. He was there, either as a patron or employee. It didn't matter to her where he worked now; he still made her smile.

She wondered how her life might be different if it hadn't mattered to her then. If she'd married Jake, she wouldn't be showering in a custom stall, watering ferns from a balcony, or buying storefront property to open a fabric shop. But she would have someone who always came to her bed, and she wouldn't need a cigarette after her morning shower.

Next to the planters she found the food spikes. After peeling back the wrappers she stuck one into each pot hanging on the rails. Some green was still there, and she hoped the plant food might help. Then she added a spike to each of the new plants. She knew she lacked a green thumb, and her neglect was likely the reason for the poor shape of the ferns. Then she decided.

Leaning back over the rails, she removed the withered plants and hung the new ferns out in the sun. She knelt down on the deck of the balcony, searching through the wilted, parched leaves, finding and removing the food spikes, then adding them to the new plants. There was no need to waste any more effort on the dying ferns; what was left would wilt under the late summer sun regardless of her efforts.

She remembered Dan in his recliner downstairs. Walking back inside, she glanced at the clock. After wrapping herself in her robe, she removed a warm towel from the clothes dryer in the laundry room and made her way to the staircase. The oak treads always felt cold on her feet, so she slipped on her house shoes. Halfway down the curving stairs she could see into the den and hear the television.

Months ago Dan quit making any effort to control his diabetes, and on nights when he drank himself senseless, he'd sit in his custom-made recliner watching golf videos rather than struggle his way up the stairs to their bed. His ability to do anything once he came to bed had ended years ago, and the drinking and diabetes were combining to shorten his life. So he'd ordered the recliner. On the left hand side was a built-in bar, including a water-proof ice-box that when filled could last him all day and night. On the right was a cabinet that held a decanter of scotch and three glasses. The recliner made him comfortable and made it easier for him to feed his addiction—effectively and efficiently ending his life.

Karen sometimes wondered if Dan believed he was doing this for her. She was still young, and his wealth would enable her to live any life she chose. He'd even suggested she buy a place in New York and go there in order to be closer to the world of fashion. That life would be on hold until he died. She held no grudges over this fact. Dan had been good to her, and her oath had been to God to care for him until death. She would fulfill that oath, and time would heal all wounds. As a registered nurse, she knew well what Dan was doing to his body, and silently acquiesced, a not-so-willing accomplice to the charade intended to end his life so hers could move forward.

Two years into retirement and twenty years into the bottle, Dr. Dan didn't care where she went or what she did, as long as the scotch cabinet was stocked with twenty-year-old single-malt and his bucket was full of ice. He hadn't always been an alcoholic, but now that he no longer had to worry about late night calls to the hospital, he could lose himself in the bottle and not worry about Karen. He had accomplished all his goals: a successful medical practice; a comfortable retirement; a golf handicap; a young, trophy wife; and a drinking problem. Now all he had to do was sit alone in his chair at night and wait for death so he could leave a wealthy young widow behind. Then he would have accomplished his final goal. They had no children. All he'd accumulated would go to Karen when he died. Although a few years ago any infidelity might have bothered him, he now considered her lack of interest and absence of any need for sex with him a relief.

Karen smiled. She remembered their honeymoon at a private beach house on Bimini. Dan was a fan of Hemingway, and they'd scoured the old buildings and bars on the island, searching for any clue of the man's long-ago visits. At one bar they found the initials of the author carved into the wall, barely discernible after the decades that had passed. They traveled to Andros, searching for the trolls that Dan claimed were related to his ex-wife. They fished for marlin and dived where legend held the fabled city of Atlantis once thrived. They stretched in the sun on the beach, Karen removing her top as Dan read "Islands in the Stream," Hemingway's posthumous novel inspired by Bimini and the islands surrounding it. Dan read aloud to her the scene where the youngest son caught but could not land the giant marlin, and wondered what the servant had whispered in the boy's ear while carrying the spent lad into the cabin after the epic battle. Dan marveled at Hemingway's courage—the ability to take his own life with a shotgun—and admitted he was too much of a coward to do such a thing. Then for the first and last time, he rubbed lotion on her back.

She loved Dr. Dan. She had never been unfaithful. They'd shared many cherished moments together. But Karen anticipated the time she would be alone and her life would once again be hers. With shame, she hoped the time would be soon.

She remembered the first night they'd slept together. Dan had never been good in bed. He'd openly admitted his shortcomings. But his biggest problem was his outdated view of sex—that a wife was to satisfy a husband, and her needs were of no consequence. At the time, sexual satisfaction was an easy sacrifice for the security, prestige, and lifestyle she'd acquired with her marriage to a doctor 25 years her senior. When she was 30, the difference didn't matter. But that didn't remove her yearnings, and now at 45, she realized all she'd missed in life. Still, she believed she could have it all, eventually. Soon.

For years, Dan had been obsessive, fanatically jealous, accusing her every time she walked out the door of meeting with nameless men in unlit parking lots and spending nights in hotels that rented rooms by the hour. But Dan finally apologized to her. He had hired a private investigator to follow her for six months, and the P.I. found no evidence of infidelity. Karen had been furious when Dan told her about the investigator. Dr. Dan had been paying for his scurrilous accusations ever since, and the financing of the fabric shop was the newest installment.

Now, as he waited for death, he just didn't care.

Karen left the staircase and walked into the den where he sat, with his feet propped on a leather bench, the empty bottle of scotch on the end table. He rarely leaned back in the recliner, as doing so made it difficult for him to drink. She kneeled and massaged his calves in an effort to help improve the circulation. If he didn't quit the drinking, he would soon lose his feet. The tips of his toes had changed in color from a light blue to a darker, more menacing shade of black. She rubbed them gingerly, then wrapped them in the towel she'd warmed in the clothes dryer. As she rose, she leaned over and kissed his forehead. Then she took the ice bucket from the recliner into the kitchen where she washed and sterilized it and refilled it with ice. After tossing the empty into the trash, she opened the liquor cabinet and removed the last bottle.

"You're out of scotch," she said. "I'll pick some up while I'm out today." She left the new bottle on the end table, well within his reach. She knew he'd want his usual breakfast, so she took a clean glass, added some ice and poured him a drink.

As she leaned over to kiss his forehead, her robe fell open, exposing her breasts. He leaned away, looking past her at the golf tournament on the television.

"Why are you going to Delbert today? You can't do your kind of shopping at that shit-hole of a town," Dan said.

"I'm thinking of buying or leasing one of the downtown storefronts for my fabric shop. The space over there is much cheaper than here in Jonesboro, or even in Success," Karen said.

"It's cheaper because they can't give them away. That town is dead. When they built that quake-proof building and moved the courthouse to Success, Delbert just died."

"That may be so, but I think a good fabric shop is like a good restaurant. People will come no matter where it is."

"How much are they asking for it?"

"I think I can get the building for somewhere between two to three hundred thousand."

"For a building in Delbert?" He took a long sip of scotch. "When the earthquake hits, that whole town square will be flattened. Make sure you get insurance to cover that, replacement cost coverage."

"The cheapest commercial space I could find on the square in Success was over a half million for a third of the square footage. I didn't even bother to price anything here."

"Well, I promised you I'd do this. I'd rather you leased for a year with an option to buy to see if this will work, but use your best judgment. Maybe that earthquake will hit and flatten the place so you can build a new one wherever you want." He took a sip from the drink Karen had prepared for him. "If you go to Campbell's bring me back one of their cheeseburgers. And some fries."

"I'm going there for breakfast this morning. That's where I'm meeting the owner," Karen said. "Jenny has the day off and is supposed to meet us for breakfast. She said she'd go look at the building with me. I may spend the night with her and the twins, so I'll have to get your burger and fries tomorrow on my way out of town.

They'll be cold by the time I get home. Is there anything else you might need before I go?"

"Campbell's fries always nuke well in the micro-wave. I can't tell the difference. Have a good time, just bring me some burgers back whenever you come home. If you get down to Wink's, tell him I said hello."

"I asked Miranda to come by tonight, and to check on you in the morning," Karen said. "She said she'd bring you something for supper."

"What about my scotch?"

"You'll be out before I get back, so I'll call her before I leave and ask her to pick up a bottle. I'll leave some cash for her on the kitchen table.

He grunted while sipping his drink. "Hey, bring me back a newspaper, too. I heard that boy I delivered years ago with the fucked up foot committed suicide. I want to see if they have any news on that."

She climbed the stairs and walked to the bedroom, removed her robe, and glanced at the mirror one more time. After getting dressed, she packed the outfit she had selected for that evening at Wink's—a tight-fitting blouse with a buckskin skirt that stretched thin over her hips and rode high on her thighs. Tonight Larry Mahan boots would replace white patent heels by Prada, and tequila shots would replace French merlot. Jake would not replace Dan, not anytime soon. But seeing him would ease her pain, and holding him as they danced tonight would stir her yearnings for all that awaited, for all the new memories they might make.

Selecting the bottle of perfume, she sprayed her body again— and inhaled, and remembered.

Perception >Reality

He walked up onto the front porch and rang the doorbell. The house seemed pleasant enough, with red brick along the front and wood siding painted olive green down the sidewalls and on the soffits. Sections of the fascia had rotted and needed replacing. The new coat of paint covered the weathered areas well, however, and gave proof the owners had decided to wait another year before replacing the rotten trim. Randy Johnson waited for someone to open the door while he admired the simple elegance of the home.

A man appeared behind the screen. Randy saw the man was not much bigger than himself, which was good, although size meant nothing.

"Are you Mr. Merriwether?" Randy adjusted his tie and waited for the man's response.

"Yes," he said.

"My name is Randy Johnson. I am the attorney appointed to represent the man charged with raping your daughter. You are under no obligation to speak to me, and if you ran me off your porch with a shotgun right now, well, I might do the same. But I'd like to speak to you about this case, if you could spare a few moments of your time."

"Clara is gone to school right now," Mr. Merriwether said.

"I know. I wanted to speak to you and your wife, if you have the time." Randy watched as Mr. Merriwether looked at his clothes and his briefcase. When interviewing witnesses Randy usually wore a suit: today he wore Levis and a button-down Oxford shirt. But this day was different. These people were not witnesses.

After a few moments hesitation, Mr. Merriwether opened the screen door and waved the attorney in.

"Would you like some coffee, Mr. Johnson?"

Randy nodded and sat down in the recliner next to the front door. This wasn't the first time Randy had chosen a seat in a room because of its proximity to an exit, and every time he did so, he reconsidered his chosen profession. An indigent appointment from the circuit court paid $500 for a case that Randy would have charged a

$5000 retainer just to get started, and here he sat, risking his life, for $500.

Mr. Merriwether brought him coffee, forgetting to ask if he wanted any cream or sugar. The old man seemed nearly as nervous as the attorney.

"Would you give me just a moment to get my wife? She's still upstairs."

"Of course," Randy said.

He wanted to jump up and run through the front door and escape with his life. Randy wondered if the old man was going upstairs to get a gun. In tomorrow's paper the headlines would read: *Attorney Slain by Victim's Father.* And no one would care. The only people who cared about one less defense attorney were the hoodlums who needed one every other week. They believed they could do whatever they wanted, pay their lawyer $500 and not even pay court costs. They didn't understand that cutting their losses was the only thing an attorney could do in most cases.

Like this one.

Looking around the room he saw pictures of the girl his client had engaged in sexual relations with before she turned fifteen. Her name was Clara, but she didn't look like any fourteen-year-old Randy had ever seen. As he shifted to rise and look at the picture, he heard noise from the stairs. If Merriwether had gone upstairs to get a gun, Randy knew he was better off seated than ogling a picture of the man's daughter.

"This is my wife, Amber. I thought she might need to sit in on this conversation," said Mr. Merriwether.

"Of course," said Randy as he rose and stepped forward to shake the lady's hand.

"I wish I could say it was a pleasure to meet you. I know why you are here; I just don't understand your purpose," Amber said.

"Well, I promise I'm not here to talk about the predicted earthquake," Randy said as he sat back down.

The Merriwethers both laughed nervously.

"Everyone seems to be getting ready for an apocalypse, but we've been so busy getting counseling for Clara and trying to deal with this situation we haven't even had time to consider it, " Amber said. "I think I have one case of bottled water stored. I gotta get some more."

"If that earthquake hits we'll all be eating Velveeta and Spam sandwiches for weeks," Randy said. He shifted uneasily in his seat before he spoke again. "Jimmie Cupp, the prosecuting attorney for this district, has a policy that he will accept any plea agreed to by the victims. I'm here to talk to you about the possibility of a plea for Tony Landis. I have no problems with you tape recording everything that we say here, because I won't say anything I wouldn't repeat in open court. But I wanted to talk to you about the case and make sure you knew everything that I knew before you made your decisions. If you will talk about this with me, I'll continue. If not, I promise I'll get up and leave and there will be no hard feelings."

"We'd like to hear what you have to say, Mr. Johnson," Amber said as she sat on the sofa next to her husband. "No one will talk to us at the sheriff's office, and we can never catch the prosecutor when he isn't in court."

"Have you seen the police report about what happened?" Randy pulled a copy of the report from his file and offered it to Amber.

"No. We haven't. All we know is what Clara has told us," Amber said. She took the paper. Randy watched as her eyes trailed along the lines of the report. The color drained from her face.

"Apparently, Tony, his wife, and Nancy, her younger sister; the Jackson girl, and your daughter, Clara, all piled up in bed that afternoon with nothing better to do. Clara was the only one that was fourteen. The other girls were sixteen and eighteen, and of course his wife is eighteen. When Tony finally wore out and could do nothing more, the girls took turns with each other as he watched."

"The deputy who wrote this seems to have enjoyed describing the events in some detail," Amber said as she handed the report to her husband.

"Apparently so," Randy said. "He even asked my client what brand of cologne he wore that day."

The room fell silent as Mr. Merriwether read things about his daughter that no man should ever know. Randy sat in his chair and waited. He had done this before—seeking out the victims of the crimes his clients had committed—asking their approval for the plea bargains he negotiated with the prosecuting attorney. This was the first time he had done so for a rape charge. Knowing the acts were consensual—and illegal only because of the age of the girl involved—gave Randy a boldness that he would have lacked had the crime been one of violence. He still felt as though he were shattering their world once more.

He could also believe he was doing the right thing; but if this were right, why did his sweaty palms grip the arms of the La-Z-Boy? If the case went to trial, Clara Merriwether's willingness to engage sexually with the girls in that bed gave Randy an opportunity to focus attention on the victim instead of his client. The prosecuting attorney had refused to charge anyone else even though two other participants in the orgy were old enough to face charges. Randy knew he could portray his client as the victim, if he could seat a jury full of men with no daughters.

Was his client his only responsibility? Randy did not want to see the Merriwether girl punished for pursuing her sexuality. He remembered the first time he had been with a man—the shame and confusion he felt. He could only imagine if the experience had been revealed in a court of law.

Exposing the Merriwethers to their daughter's activities—expanding their realm of knowledge as Randy called it—would benefit both his client and the victim, if a trial could be avoided. But did the Merriwethers truly need to know all that had happened? What if someone felt that Randy's wife, Monica, should know about his affair? The lies he told and the efforts he made to cover up his weakness? The money he was about to spend to take his red-headed secretary to Cancun so he could meet with Cameron, the male prostitute he had met in Boston? Monica's world seemed perfect to her, and Randy's law partners all believed he was having an affair with Macie, his secretary; and wasn't the perception more important than the reality? Being exposed for an affair with his secretary would ruin his marriage, but exposure of his bisexuality would cost him his practice.

Maybe Randy sought the approval of these parents because he knew too well the addiction their daughter suffered. He loved his wife. He shook his head after the thought. Yes. He loved her. But he loved himself more, and he knew he could never settle for sex with a woman. Maybe he wanted the Merriwethers to give Clara the approval he would never receive.

"I have not been told of any of this," Mr. Merriwether said after he finished reading the report.

"If this case goes to trial, all of this will come out. I am sitting here in your living room having a nice conversation with you, and you might even think I am a nice man. But I'm more like a rattlesnake that's quit rattling. That doesn't mean I won't still bite. When this goes to trial, I will offer testimony that your daughter went down on everyone in that bed, not just the man charged with statutory rape. She had oral sex with three other girls, and allowed them to have oral sex with her. I was pretty sure the sheriff's department hadn't told you about this."

Amber leaned over toward her husband and reached out to squeeze his hand. "No. They did not tell us about this, or even let us see this report. This would have been a complete surprise."

"If I am forced to take this to trial, you are going to hate me. I will have a field day with this report. All of the girls gave statements admitting what went on, so there is no way anyone will be able to lie. We'll spend more time in court going over what happened between the three girls than we'll spend talking about what my client did. And I have already sent a letter to the prosecutor asking him why the girls who had sexual contact with your daughter were not charged with statutory rape. After all, two of them were eighteen. Both of them are guilty of the same crime my client is charged with, and the two sisters should have been charged with incest."

"But your client had sexual intercourse with our daughter," Mr. Merriwether said. "How can the two eighteen-year-old girls be charged with rape?"

"Under Arkansas law, what the girls did is legally defined as deviant sexual activity. That carries the same penalty as intercourse. I have a copy of the statute, and I would encourage you to go see Mr. Cupp and ask him, or even better, go see your own attorney and make sure that everything I am telling you is the truth."

"I promise you, Mr. Johnson, we plan to do exactly that," Amber said. "Because I just don't see how we can trust you. How do we know your intentions? You act like you are concerned for our daughter, but your only goal is to get your client off."

"My client will not walk away from this, Amber. He will go to prison. Many times, practicing law is not about winning or losing. It's about cutting your losses. My brother has a daughter just a few years younger than Clara. Our children are sexual beings and will experiment and make mistakes. Those mistakes are usually family secrets, buried deep within the memory of the one who walked in and caught them as they experimented after school with their boyfriend or girlfriend when they thought no one was home. But when that happens, parents counsel or punish or try to educate their children; the incident is never published."

Randy leaned forward to emphasize his point.

"This is a mistake in judgment for all of these kids. My client is just eighteen. He had his wife and her own sister in bed with him. His wife watched as he had sex with her sister, then she did the same. They both watched as the other girls—"

"We read the report. I know what went on. Get to your point, Mr. Johnson," Amber said.

"These mistakes are about to make the front page of the daily newspaper."

"What can we do?" Mr. Merriwether leaned forward and offered the report back to the attorney.

"You can cut your losses, too. Here is the plea I propose. My client will plead guilty to one count of rape. That charge is a Y felony that has a ten-year minimum sentence. He will be sentenced to serve ten years."

"Right, but he won't serve ten years. How much will he serve?" Amber leaned forward in her chair as she asked her question. "By the way, Mr. Johnson, can I get you some more coffee?"

"Please," Randy said as he offered her his cup.

"Don't stop now," she said as she walked into the kitchen. "I can hear you just fine."

"Under normal circumstances, he'd serve a year. With this being a "Y" Felony, he'll serve 25% of his time before he's eligible for parole. The other charge will be merged into this one."

"What other charges were there?' Amber brought his coffee and set it down in front of him.

"He was charged with one count of carnal abuse for his actions with the seventeen-year-old girl. Her age kept it from being rape, but also kept it from being legal."

Mr. Merriwether leaned back in his chair and ran his hand through his hair. "What have the other parents agreed to?"

"The father of my client's wife, and his wife's sister, is a deputy at the sheriff's office. He is happy with the deal and has already signed off on it. So has the mother of the other girl. Their names and telephone numbers are listed on the back of that report. You can call them and ask them anything you'd like to know."

"I know rape trials are hard on the victims," Amber said.

"They are hard enough when the victim hasn't been as actively engaged as your daughter. I have a video I want to leave you of a movie titled *The Accused*. Watch it tonight, without your daughter. Your daughter doesn't need to see this until you have a chance to decide for yourself if it's suitable for her. But this movie will give you an idea of what goes on. Your daughter is a victim here, but when I get started in that courtroom, she will be anything but a victim."

"If you are so reluctant to do this to my daughter," Amber said, "Then why do you do this for a living?"

Randy picked up the cup of coffee, and as he took his final sip, he carefully thought of a good answer to her question.

"I was a Deputy Prosecutor up in Sharp County, and I worked closely with the Department of Human Services on child molestation cases. The case worker up there asked me the same question after I moved out and began a private practice. She asked me how I could represent these people."

He set the cup down and stood. "The only way to become a successful lawyer is to win and be successful on cases like this."

"Then why come to us? Why not go to trial and win your big case? Prove my daughter is a lesbian? Get your name in the papers so you can handle more rape cases and make more money," Amber said.

108

Randy gathered his things as if he were preparing to leave. "I told that caseworker she could go to bed at night and sleep, because the lawmen of this state knew that when they came to court, I'd be there waiting for them, to make sure they did everything by the book. I don't do it for them. I do it for every other law abiding citizen who will ever need me."

Mr. Merriwether stood. "Bullshit. Do you expect me to believe that?"

"No. I don't. But I sure don't take these appointments for the money," Randy said as he stood and picked up his briefcase. "Maybe it's best that even I don't know why I do this. It's my job; my chosen profession. It's too late to go back to school and become a doctor, so I have to do the best I can with the cards I'm dealt. I can't change who and what I am. And then, I have to try to sleep at night, which sometimes isn't easy."

"We'll let you know what we decide," Amber said as they walked him to the door.

Randy walked out the door and got into his Chevy Blazer. He would wait for word from the Merriwethers before he spoke to his client about this meeting. As he drove away, he looked again at the house. From the road he couldn't tell the trim was rotting and about to fall down. Whoever painted that house knew well how to hide the dry-rot and termite infested wood. If Mr. Merriwether would still speak to him after this ordeal ended, he might ask for the name of the contractor.

Penumbra

When Monica Chamberlain lived in Boston, she hung out at the airport. As the travelers scurried about their journeys, she watched, and she heard their words and saw their actions as potential fodder for the complicated crossword puzzles she wrote and eventually sold to *The New York Times* or *The Boston Globe*. Everything they said or did appeared to her as an intersection: four letter word for *late plane*, connect on the third letter with a ten letter word for *misplaced baggage*, connect on the sixth letter with a seven letter word for *a tearful reunion*. When she waited for someone, as she did now at the Memphis International Airport, she arrived early and sat and listened to the conversations around her. She loved to find new words with old meanings, and her hobby provided a welcome distraction from the dreaded meeting with her older sister.

Beginnings and endings seemed the most difficult parts of drafting a crossword puzzle for Monica. If she happened to spell a word wrong, she messed up the whole graph, so she never connected the words on the first or last letter until she knew exactly how many blanks were needed. Airport bookstores never carried a good dictionary—a good one was too big to carry around—so she filled her pages then rushed home to her etymology dictionary or an OED and drafted the clues.

Older than Monica by three years, Grace Chamberlain competed with her younger sister for everything that touched their lives. Grace went to Harvard; Monica attended Boston College. Grace was engaged to a Harvard doctor; Monica married an Arkansas lawyer. Grace performed volunteer work at the Harvard Medical Center; Monica wrote and sold crossword puzzles and lived off her share of the substantial dividends she received from the latex patent her family owned.

Grace had introduced Monica to Randy—the cute lawyer with the bad southern accent—during an American Bar Association convention in Boston. Monica went to discover new words for her puzzles, and Grace tagged along to find a great lay. Monica's sister bragged she would fuck Randy before the night was over. Grace worked hard to seduce Randy, but he only saw Monica. She did her best to ignore him, but Monica woke-up in his bed the next morning. Although the rest of her family never understood, she knew why her sister refused to attend her wedding.

Monica sat at gate 25 and checked the status board for flight 376 arriving from Boston. As she waited, she heard the conversation of a couple arriving from Mexico. Men, women, and children moved about her, and she opened her pad of graph paper to its second page. The joy of the people as they walked through the gate and found those who waited for them always fascinated her. She remembered the surprised look on her husband's face, on Randy's face. She had to stop thinking of him as her husband. When he got off the plane from Cancun with his secretary, the court appointed process server hired by her attorney served Randy with the divorce papers, and the secretary with a restraining order keeping her away from Monica and the house. Monica had waved at Randy just as he looked up from the summons. Outside of court proceedings, they hadn't spoken to each other since that day.

After serving papers on Randy and his secretary at the airport, Monica had called Grace and told her about Randy's affair and the pending divorce. She asked her sister to break the news to the family.

It wasn't hard to imagine Grace talking to the family in Boston, telling them she knew all along the boy was out for a share of Monica's substantial inheritance. "Nothing but white trash" was a phrase Grace loved to use after the night they met him. Grace had refused to attend the wedding, claiming she couldn't leave her volunteer position at the Harvard Medical Center to fly to Arkansas for the hillbilly affair. Monica's childhood dreams of her wedding always included her sister at her side. The photographer never understood why the bride refused to pose with her maids for any pictures.

The meeting, at the airport with her ex-husband, had happened just a few weeks earlier. Randy had caved, granting all of her requests, and the divorce was quickly over. The yard sale would be next.

Monica saw and heard the people moving and talking, the travelers, businessmen and women, who arrived and rented cars, or made themselves comfortable for layovers always longer than expected. She filled the graph paper before her with words. Most of the time she didn't know the meaning of the words she used, selecting an overheard tidbit for its mysterious sound, or because of the way it rolled off her tongue when she pronounced it. Although she heard many new words, there were few she couldn't understand by listening to their context. *Penumbra* was a new one she would have to look up.

When she lived at home, in Boston, she would take a dictionary to the bathroom with her, and after running a tub full of steaming hot water, she soaked and searched the pages for words. She sold her first puzzle on her eighteenth birthday and had sold enough since that day to make two thick books. Always classified as difficult, her crosswords were never as complicated as her older sister.

Monica looked up from her graph paper and saw Grace coming up the ramp, wheeling a suitcase behind her as she searched the faces of the crowd for her ride. Their eyes met; Grace smiled.

Monica walked to Grace and took her in her arms, squeezing her. Grace dropped the handle on her luggage and squeezed Monica tight, smoothing the long black hair that flowed down over Monica's back. The difficult explanations Grace would demand, the condescending scolding Monica would receive, all the baggage Grace brought with her, couldn't keep Monica from sobbing as Grace held her.

"So what was that red-headed bitch wearing when they got off the plane?"

"I don't remember, Grace. I'm sure it was warm when they left Cancun, but they'd dressed for the cooler weather."

"I bet his little dick shriveled like a smelt when he saw you."

"Let's get out of here," Monica said.

"I'm sorry, sis. If you don't want to talk about it, that's fine." Grace bent to pick up the handle on her luggage, but Monica had it, and with her arm through Grace's mink coat, Monica led her sister toward the exit.

"I don't mind talking. You're the first person I can talk to about it. I have a bunch of new words. Got to get the OED to look them up."

"What did you hear while you were waiting?"

"*Penumbra, Queerencia,* and *Wegener Hypothesis.*"

"Oh, I know the hypothesis thing," Grace said. "That's a theory that the land masses were all attached at one time and then separated and slowly drifted apart over the eons."

"Sounds more like our parents than the continents. There is the gate where we met them," Monica said.

"We?"

"I had the process server with me, Jimmy. Arkansas requires a certified process server. Let me show you." Monica guided Grace over and explained how she came to Memphis that day with the divorce papers and the summons for her husband.

"Did you see her?"

"I know who she is. She's worked in his office now for years."

"I didn't know that. All you told me was that he'd cheated on you and you were getting a divorce. We haven't exactly been speaking to each other lately."

"I drew the bitch's name last year at the office Christmas party. Can you believe I bought her lingerie because she was single? I drove to all the way to Little Rock to find something to fit her."

"I want to drive by Graceland on the way out. I heard it's small," Grace said. "Mother told me about your yard sale."

"You'd be proud of me. I am not going be like Mom and tolerate this shit. As soon as I knew what he was doing, I took action. You wouldn't believe the small town bullshit. It was impossible to get an attorney from anywhere but Little Rock, not a fucking one of them would represent me. They all know him and have practiced with him or against him at one time or another. What's so funny about it, to hear Randy talk, he wouldn't hire any of them to represent a dog."

"Mom stayed with Dad because we are Catholic. You are Catholic, Monica. Have you thought about what you are doing?"

Monica stopped and looked at her sister. Always full of surprises, Grace never failed to keep her off balance.

"You are not suggesting I stay with him."

"No, I'm not, not really. Are we going to see Graceland before we leave?"

The drive from Memphis to Delbert passed quickly as they talked about their old friends from Boston. Monica soon pulled into the driveway of her home and turned the keys in the ignition. She pulled the lever on the side of the seat; the trunk lid popped open.

"You live here?" Grace asked.

"You've got to stop comparing everything. This is my home, and I love it here."

Immaculate by Delbert standards, the one story red brick home with the low-pitched roof and rusted aluminum windows would never compare to their family estate in Boston.

"I didn't settle for this. I chose this, and in spite of all that's happened, I still don't want to leave."

"I haven't seen you since you got married," Grace said. "Five years. I'm not here to criticize, I promise. Fathead."

"Get your own luggage, bitch," Monica said. They laughed and got out of the car. As they walked to the garage, Grace looked at the backyard, filled with items placed in organized rows for a yard sale. Grace stopped.

"Everything is five dollars?"

Monica had the keys in the back door. Without looking back at Grace, she said, "That's how many years we were together."

"When is the earthquake supposed to hit? I read this is the center of the New Madrid fault, and that Indian guy says there will be an earthquake. Do you have insurance for that?"

They walked into the house, and Monica hung her keys from the hook on a plaque that read "Home Sweet Home." The plaque was a Christmas present from her in-laws and would not be placed in the yard sale.

"How did you hear about the earthquake?"

"I read about it in the papers, or some magazine, I don't remember. Where do I sleep? I hope you don't have any silverfish here."

"No silverfish; just a few scorpions," Monica said as she began to prepare supper.

114

***

After breakfast the next morning they went to the backyard and finished organizing all the items for sale. Monica had most everything the way she wanted, so she spent most of the morning telling Grace the history behind the inventory. The yard held three boats, a long narrow twenty foot john boat used for trout fishing at Gaston's Resort on the White River, a big cabin cruiser Randy had used to run hunters to the duck blind over at the Hatchie Coon Bottoms, and a Ranger bass boat with a huge Black Max Mercury outboard they had used on Norfork Lake. A twenty-foot Air Stream camper sat along the back fence, and a Star-Craft pop-up filled the space behind it. A Polaris four-wheeler occupied the concrete slab next to the deck that surrounded the back door.

A Webber gas grill stood a few feet from the patio doors. "Is that for sale too, or built in?" asked Grace.

"He ran a propane line from that big tank out back." Monica pointed at a huge tank that sat off to the side in the back yard. "It's attached. I can't get rid of it."

"Remember the lemonade stands we used to have? We couldn't sell a glass of lemonade to save our souls. I know why now. I can just hear those people in Father's neighborhood. *Look at the little rich bitches. Always hustling for another dollar*. I'd hate to have a lemonade stand in this neighborhood."

"The girls in the 4-H club had a stand here once a week this past summer and made over two thousand dollars to attend their regional meeting," Monica said. "People here would give them as much as five dollars for a cup of lemonade. The girls were giving it away, just asking for a donation for camp."

"Ha. You couldn't have done that in Boston. Those greedy bastards would have drunk every drop and not left a penny," Grace said.

"I don't know. I didn't really know what to expect when I came down here, but I think people are people, no matter where they are from."

"We never made more than five bucks, ever, with our stand."

"We weren't doing it for a charitable cause, just for us."

"Where's the rest of the stuff?"

"Everything else is inside the garage."

They walked up onto the deck and Grace took a seat. From inside the kitchen, they heard a whistling sound.

"Is that a tea-pot?"

"Been a while since I had hot tea down here. They always want to put ice in it. I'll be right back." Monica went through the sliding glass doors and disappeared inside the house. Grace left the deck and inspected the Polaris four-wheeler.

Monica returned with a silver tray. The strings from the bags of Earl Grey tea dangled over the sides of the English Regency Eggshell Georgian teacups.

"Isn't that Mother's pattern?"

"This doesn't go in the yard sale," Monica said. "Neither do those Browning shotguns I have set by the front door."

"You had me wondering about the neighborhood when I saw those guns."

"Those belonged to Randy's father. They were made in Belgium and are some kind of a special gun to these guys down here. I'd never heard of them before, but I'm taking them back."

"Dad gave this pattern to Mother for their anniversary. I can't even remember which one."

"The one when he announced we had a baby brother not living with us. That's probably the reason it's here in Arkansas." Monica sat and took the saucer with the cup and sipped the tea. She laughed and nearly choked. "I'm sorry," she said to Grace as she grabbed a napkin from the service tray to clean up. "I was just thinking about the first time I met Randy's parents, how they slurped at their coffee. I had to leave the room to compose myself. But God, they are the most incredible people you will ever meet."

"I'm sure they have their faults."

"He never cheated on his wife," Monica said.

"You don't know that."

"Dad never made an effort to stop. I am not waiting on Randy to decide."

"Mother never believed it was right to leave," Grace said. "Catholics don't divorce."

"Mother refused to believe the truth, and she was no different from these people here. She didn't want to leave the money. She made her choice and then wanted everyone to feel sorry for her."

"If she'd divorced Father, she'd have had all the money she needed."

"It wouldn't have been the same, Grace. She couldn't have traveled in the same social circles afterward. She didn't want to give that up." Monica set her cup and saucer down on the glass top of the table. "Don't try to tell me she stayed because of her religion. I don't feel sorry for her. Mother was more concerned about the china on which she served her guests than who Father had fucked the night before."

"Dad always favored you. How can you talk about him like this now?"

"His favors were bribes, Grace. I caught him in his office screwing some woman I'd never seen before, the day before my thirteenth birthday. He looked right at me, and I eased back out of the room."

"Are you sure he saw you?" Grace nearly dropped her teacup. She leaned forward across the table as if her sister had whispered the words.

"He looked right at me. And when he came home, he had a brand new puppy for me. Remember how I always wanted a dog and we couldn't have one because of Mother's allergies?"

"What did he say to you?"

"That still has me pissed off. He never one time tried to talk to me or explain what had happened. He just assumed he could buy my silence without even asking for it."

"I never knew. That explains the Corvette for your sixteenth birthday. That explains a lot, Monica. But I still want you to think about the religious consequences of what you are doing," Grace said.

"I thought about it before I had my first abortion, and I did it anyway. I don't think divorcing a cheating husband will put me in a worse position with the church."

A flock of snow geese flew overhead, their cries disturbing the silence between them. The sisters sat and watched and listened. The cries of the white birds with the black-tipped wings could be heard long after they passed out of sight. "Those geese fly north to mate. I came south."

"You didn't exactly wait till you got here, Monica. I never knew you had an abortion. Why didn't you tell me?"

"Twice. Two abortions. You weren't interested, and I knew I couldn't trust you not to use the situation against me. You just had to be better than me. It's like Graceland. You didn't want to see it. You wanted to bitch about how small it was."

"It is small," Grace said.

"You could have been here for my wedding," Monica said.

Grace set her cup and saucer on the table. She walked over to her sister and bent to hug her. "Do you know how to run that four-wheeler? I've never been on one."

"Get those guns and we'll take them over to my in-laws. We'll put them in that rack there on the front," Monica said. "You might as well meet them. You'll never get another chance."

After loading the guns onto the metal rack on the front of the Polaris, the two sisters climbed on board. Monica started the four-wheeler and nearly dumped Grace off the back as they raced down the street and cut through a freshly plowed field. After delivering the guns, Monica and Grace rode on the four-wheeler till they were covered in mud.

***

Monica didn't know for sure where she would go, but she knew she couldn't be present for the sale. Before leaving the next morning, she gave Grace simple instructions. "Everything is to be sold." The boats, the four-wheeler, the campers, all the larger items that lined the yard. The diamond rings, the herringbone necklaces, the useless junk bought from Pier One Imports in Little Rock, the handmade Amish bedroom suite they ordered in Branson, and the Weatherby bolt-action rifles that lined the walls of the garage. There were no price tags. Everything was five dollars.

Monica Chamberlain—she had refused to change her name after they married—had advertised the sale in last Wednesday's weekly edition of *The Delbertian*. She gave Grace a copy of the ad before she left that morning. Unlike the normal ads placed under the "Rummage Sale" section of the classifieds, Monica's block ad covered two bottom quarter columns of the back page of the paper, just like the ones used by auctioneers to give notice of estate liquidations. In big block letters a heading read: "Randy Johnson/Monica Chamberlain Divorce Sale; Nothing over $5.00." A long list of items filled the columns of the ad.

Monica went over the list with Grace one last time.

The crowd began to arrive early, although the ad stated no sales would be made before seven o'clock. When Monica left that morning at six, cars lined both sides of the street, and people had parked all the way around the block. Jess McCord, the accountant who did their taxes and gave a deposition about the value of Randy Johnson's interest in the White law firm, sat astride the big Polaris four-wheeler next to the Ranger bass boat. He might not be able to buy it before seven, but he sure wasn't going to let anyone else beat him to it. Monica saw the pile of cigarette butts on the ground next to the Polaris and figured the man must have been there all night.

"Jess, you pick up every one of those cigarette butts before you leave my yard."

"I'm sorry, Monica. I didn't even think about it," Jess said. He climbed off the Polaris and collected the butts, stuffing them in his coat pocket as he fumbled through the grass to find them all.

The Lexus wasn't for sale, so Monica started it up and pulled out of the driveway. Campbell's Café was just a few blocks away, so she decided to spend the morning there rather than leave town for the day.

Downtown had changed a bit that morning. On the south side of the square, just two doors down from Campbell's Café and right next to McHaney's Hardware, the employees of Lavelle's Billboard Company from Success, Arkansas, worked on removing the White, Foulkes and Long Law Firm sign. They replaced it with a new one, White, Foulkes, Long and Johnson. The changing of the sign, along with the yard sale, could commence since the divorce was over.

Massive white oaks lined the town square of Delbert, Arkansas, and the leaves had emerged from what, days ago, were swollen buds at the ends of long branches. Dogwoods and redbuds blossomed along the city streets, and conical yellow Easter lilies bloomed in every vacant lot. Monica parked up the street from the White law firm, locked her car—a habit she still followed from her days in Boston—and stepped up on the sidewalk. She inhaled the fragrant spring breeze.

After pausing long enough to buy a copy of the *Arkansas Democrat* from a machine on the street corner, Monica walked to Campbell's Café where she opened the door and walked in. A wooden booth stained to a dark walnut hue hugged the east wall in the middle of the cafeteria. She hadn't worked on her puzzles since she met Grace at the airport. After taking a seat, she pulled from her bag a *Merriam-Webster's Pocket Dictionary* and a pad of graph paper. She'd check her edits against the OED later when she got home.

A middle-aged waitress with *Jenny* printed on a nametag appeared at the booth with a mug. She placed it on the table and filled it with steaming coffee.

"Haven't seen you here before, Mrs. Johnson. Can I get you something for breakfast?" Jenny set the coffee pot down on the table as she pulled a small order pad from one of her pockets. Monica heard the tip change rattle in Jenny's apron as she took her first sip of coffee.

"I have never been Mrs. Johnson."

Jenny leaned over Monica's table. "I'm sorry. I don't know your first name, and I hadn't heard whether you took your maiden name after the divorce. Just trying to be polite. I promise."

Monica looked up at Jenny and smiled. "I never changed my name. Did you not see my ad? It has my maiden name listed."

"No, I don't read the paper. Don't usually need to with working up here," Jenny said. "But I heard about your big liquidation today."

"Why aren't you at my yard sale?"

"Are you kidding? I couldn't get off from work, and Glen didn't even need me this morning. Everyone in the county must be there. Sure been dead here." Jenny smiled at her, then reached out and clasped Monica's bare left hand.

"I think I'll just read my paper for a while. I've never been here before, and I wanted to see what was so special about this place."

"Well, it ain't Glen's cooking. Does that paper have one of your crosswords in it?"

"How did you know I write crosswords?"

"This isn't Boston, honey. Keep your eyes open. You're bound to hear your name this morning." Jenny topped off the cup of coffee and walked away.

"Hey. I'm Monica," she called to Jenny's back. Jenny looked back at her and winked. Monica tasted the strong, bitter coffee again and began to look through the paper. The editors of the *Arkansas Democrat* had placed the crossword puzzle next to the cartoons. The clues were simple. Hers were much more difficult. She finished the puzzle in five minutes and set it aside. The pages of her dictionary were far more interesting.

Penumbra: Shadow cast (as in an eclipse) where the light is partly but not wholly cut off by the intervening body.

Monica smiled. She could use Grace's name for the clue to that word. The letters fit perfectly in the blocks of the graph down the left side of the paper. At the bottom of the graph, she wrote *one down: overshadowed.*

She would never get used to discussing her affairs with a total stranger at the local café. The gregarious nature of small town existence wore on her, and southern life was not the idyllic picture painted by the movies and literature. She yearned for the anonymity that she'd once again achieve upon her return to Boston. Then she heard her name.

"That rubber bitch has ruined that poor bastard."

"That's one of them northern wenches for you. Fight like hell to take it all, then give it all away."

"She's an eastern wench, you idiot."

"I'm gonna bitch slap you if you call me an idiot again."

"Then don't be one. You'll be out there directing traffic like Earl if we don't keep an eye on you."

Another word caught Monica's eye.

Saphead: A weak minded, stupid person.

Just below was another word she'd never heard before.

Saponaceous: Liable to slip away. Ingratiating, but evasive.

"She's just getting even with the poor bastard. But she'll put ideas in all the women's heads if she ain't careful."

Tathagata. An enlightened one. A finder of truth.

Monica knew Wink Gaskill's voice. Wink was subpoenaed for every divorce case in Northeast Arkansas. He owned Wink's Bar and Grill out on the Highway 1 Bypass and served as a deacon at Mooney Marrs' church. Wink faithfully tithed ten percent of his net profit from the bar, the most profitable operation in the county besides the Schugtown Co-op and Cotton Gin out at Schugtown. His devotion to tithing helped head-off any wet dry referendums in the county.

The discussion came from a set of tables two rows over. Six men sat with coffee cups the waitresses constantly refilled. The back door of the café opened. Jess McCord walked in and sat with them. The loudest one, a man in bib overalls with his pant legs stuffed inside his polished but worn cowboy boots, spoke next.

"Did you get that four-wheeler, Jess?"

"That whole city block is a mad house. You'd think she was giving away commodities."

Monica smiled as she overheard the discussion. She had volunteered to help at a commodities distribution at the county fairgrounds. The line had snaked around the deserted midway two hours before they opened. Imagining her neighbors dealing with the people trying to park in their yards, she realized she would have some apologies to deliver.

"I'll give you a thousand dollars for that four-wheeler," said Sparky Hunt, the man who owned the Nickel Creek Title Company. "I'll even throw in five hundred bucks worth of firecrackers." He wore corduroy trousers and a shirt that looked like standard jail issue orange. Randy said they called him Sparky because he closed down the title company every July and ran the biggest fireworks stand in Jester County. Sparky had arranged for the Colossal Colon, a forty-foot walk through model of a male intestinal tract, to come to the Jester County Fair. He'd had two polyps removed from his own colon four years ago and knew firsthand the need for awareness of a man's intestinal health. Monica remembered him from the closing on their home. He sat on a pillow at the time.

"I'm keeping it. That sucker's brand new. Must have cost him five grand," Jess McCord said.

Four with taxes, Monica thought. She wanted breakfast now, so when Jenny walked by to refill her cup, she asked about the breakfast special.

"It's there on the poster just above your head, sweetie. Hasn't changed in years, except the price goes up every once in a while."

Monica ordered the special, two eggs, bacon, hash browns, and biscuits with gravy. She looked around the café and tried to count the phones hung on the wall. The owner of Campbell's Café collected old phones, and he lined the walls of the cafeteria with them. Many were old, crank type models, but she spotted one on a special built shelf that looked like a fax machine with a phone line that ran out the side of the box. As she watched, the machine started printing out a fax on a white sheet of paper. Monica grinned. Not everything hung on the wall was for show, although she couldn't tell the difference between the functional and the displays.

Querencia. An area in the arena taken by the bull for a defensive stand in a bullfight.

Jenny delivered Monica's breakfast. As Monica salted and peppered her eggs, the door burst open. The cafeteria became quiet. She looked up from her plate. In the door of the cafeteria stood Randy Johnson; his eyes finally found Monica, and he charged toward her. They would all know her now, but she didn't care.

"I can't believe you're doing this," he said.

"Your accountant bought your four-wheeler this morning. He's sitting right back there. Maybe he'll sell it back to you," Monica said.

Jess McCord got up from the table where he sat with the other men and slipped out the back door of the café.

"Why take it all and just give it away?"

"Did you really think I wanted it? You knew I certainly didn't need it." Monica sat and looked up at Randy. Although her coffee no longer steamed, she slowly raised the cup to her lips and gingerly sipped the black liquid. She smiled as she thought of Randy's parents. After setting her cup back on the table, she picked up her fork and returned to her breakfast. She would miss her in-laws.

"The girls had no right to be rude to Macie," he said.

"What do you mean?" Monica dropped her fork.

"Grace threatened to kick her ass. She threw a yard dart at her, Monica. Macie is down at the sheriff's office filing charges right now."

"You shouldn't have sent that red-headed whore to my yard sale."

"I didn't think you and Grace could stand each other," Randy said. "What's she doing here?"

"Did you forget about the restraining order keeping Macie off the property, too?" Monica smiled at her ex-husband. She sat upright and looked directly into Randy's eyes. The country lawyer she'd met at a Boston bar had appeared larger than life to her. But the one time she'd finally bested her sister turned out to be the biggest mistake of her life. Not because of the farce of a marriage she'd endured, but because of the strain placed on her relationship with her family.

Grace hadn't come to Arkansas to gloat, as Monica had feared. She came to be with her. Maybe Randy had served some purpose in her life.

"Grace threw a yard dart at her?" Monica's crossed legs kept time with the swish-swoosh of the ceiling fans that twirled above their heads. She would not allow herself to be beaten down like a witness on cross-examination. Her older sister in a rage was something Monica could vividly picture. Monica had experienced her sister's wrath many times before. "Did Macie try to barter with her on one of the guns?"

"She said the Brownings were already gone." Randy fumbled in his pocket for a cigarette. He stuck it his mouth and pulled out a lighter.

"This is the nonsmoking side of the cafeteria," Monica said.

"I thought the east side was the smoking side."

"It is, you idiot. That's the east side," she said as she pointed at the table of men who sat across from them, listening to every word they said. The men grabbed at forks to stir their cold eggs.

"Jesus Christ, Monica. Look back there. They're smoking on both sides of the damned room. They always have."

"Maybe. But this morning, where I sit is a no-smoking zone."

124

Randy tossed the unlit cigarette into the ashtray that sat on Monica's table. He started to ease into the other side of the dark stained booth.

"You have not been invited to join me," she said. "Now leave me the fuck alone."

"You did this to ruin me."

"Yes, Randy. That was all I thought about as I waited for you to return from Cancun. That and wondering if she was wearing the garters I bought for her last Christmas."

A loud chuckle broke the silence that had settled over the café. Randy unbuttoned the front of his blazer and pulled back the sides as he stuffed his hands into his pockets.

"Things aren't what you think. Macie is innocent in all of this. I gave you what you wanted to protect her. You'll never understand. I made a mistake, but I still love you." Stiff and quiet, he turned and walked toward the front door of Campbell's Café.

"Randy."

He stopped and looked back.

"I gave your father the Belgium Brownings," Monica said.

"Thank you." He turned and walked on out the door.

Monica took the cigarette from the ashtray and placed it in her mouth. Jenny appeared with a lighter she pulled from her tip pocket and lit the Marlboro.

"Thanks."

One of the waitresses called out an order for Glen at the back of the café and the place once again bubbled to life. Monica set the graph paper and dictionary aside. As she sipped her coffee, she looked at another empty sheet of paper.

Beginning a new crossword always provided the greatest challenge

Ferdinand C. Posey

The old man sat at one of Jenny's tables, the one close to the entrance. Not many people sat there in December because of the cold draft from the constant opening and closing of the door. Carrying a mug and a pot of coffee, Jenny approached him.

"Can I get you some breakfast, sir?" She set the mug in front of the man and filled it with steaming black coffee.

"I might get something later, ma'am," he said with a gravelly voice that sounded familiar to her. A black leather vest hung around the man's shoulders, and he wore what appeared from a distance to be black leather slacks. But the pants were vinyl and showed cracks in the material from years of wear. The rolled up sleeves of a white T-shirt revealed rows of tattoos that covered the once massive arms. Now the tattoos hung as loose as the flesh from the old man's bones. Jenny had seen jailhouse work before, but these tattoos were artistic, revealing images of sailors in the arms of mermaids, angels with massive wings hovering over a naked man mounted by a naked woman. Jenny saw other images, but she didn't want to stare. The white of his long, flowing beard matched his hair. It covered his chest and neatly blended with the long hair that fell down his back and over the front of his shoulders. A small briefcase filled the chair next to him.

The brilliant blue of his eyes seemed to be lost in the age of his face. A mesh of long thin scars ran from just above his eyebrows on up into his receding hairline. His forehead looked as if a cat had used him to sharpen its claws. He pulled a couple packets of B.C. Powder from his vest pocket. After he opened them, he dumped the contents into the coffee and then stirred until the white dust disappeared.

"Well, I guess that guy missed his earthquake prediction. I never even felt a tremor that day," he said.

"Oh, I guess only Christ himself could have got it right twice in a row. This guy ain't no Nostradamus," Jenny said. "But it's bound

126

to happen sooner or later, they say. So I guess we better get ready for it, whether we like it or not."

Jenny left him and walked around the café, re-filling coffee cups and asking if anyone needed anything else. Thanksgiving had come and gone. Christmas would arrive in just a few days.

Iben Browning had missed his prediction of a devastating earthquake that would occur along the new Madrid Fault on December 2nd of 1990.

Along with the usual Christmas activities, people seemed to have forgotten the threat of the earthquake. Chuck Powell, the Mayor of Delbert and manager of the Wallace and Owens grocery store, had done everything he could to educate the population about what they needed to be prepared for the coming disaster. He'd even created a special aisle with earthquake supplies that he'd marked down to cost. But a week after the earthquake didn't happen, Chuck was told by the corporate office to remove the display.

Macon Huckaby, the owner of the local Sears appliance store, had sold over fifty generators, setting a new record for a Sears store in a small market. He'd won a trip to Rio for his efforts. Jenny's customers at the café had joked that Macon needed to take his trip before the earthquake, that way he'd be gone when it happened. The last time Jenny had waited on Macon, he said he wished he'd taken the trip. Forty of the generators had been returned for refunds the week after the predicted date of the earthquake. Sears cancelled his trip.

Even with all the distractions, people always seemed to tip better during the holiday seasons, and Jenny tried her best to earn the little extra she made.

From the back of the room came the ring of the bell, another plate of food ready to be served. As she approached the back counter, she saw Glen staring at the old man seated near the door.

"Do you know who that is?" Glen asked. He didn't wait for her response. "That's Handsome Kenny King. He was the King of Memphis Wrestling. We watched him every Saturday back when I was a kid. He dated Etta Coffman for about a year after she won the Miss Arkansas contest. That was before she married Ralph, of course."

127

"His voice sounded familiar. But I didn't recognize him," Jenny said. "I saw a wrestling match once, back when they put on a benefit for the Children's Home. All of us kids got in free."

"He wrestled at that match. I was there. My God, Jenny. That man is famous."

"Well, I won't charge him for his coffee, then," Jenny said as she picked up the plate of breakfast between them.

"Just don't charge him for refills," Glen said to her back as she walked away.

"I gave him a refill for the first cup," Jenny said.

***

Many years ago the American Legion had sponsored wrestling matches at Delbert. Posters advertising the Saturday night matches hung from every telephone pole in town. No wonder the name sounded familiar. Jenny remembered the benefit the promoters had put on for the Children's Home. She met Austin Idol, the Superstar Billy Graham, the Fabulous Freebirds, and Dirty Dutch Mantel. Now she remembered the old man's face. The Boogie Woogie Man, Handsome Kenny King, had not been called the King of Memphis until many years later.

At the benefit put on for the Children's Home, Handsome, as Kenny King was called then, had faced the devastating power of "The Claw," a face grip used by Baron Von Raschke. No one had ever escaped "The Claw," and the only way to beat Von Raschke was to avoid being caught in his vise-like pinch. But after wrestling and avoiding the deadly hold for what seemed like an hour, Baron Von Raschke managed to clamp down on Handsome's face. Handsome Kenny King managed to fight his way up off the matt and jump over the top rope. The Baron's wrist broke and the match ended. Blood covered both of their faces as they left the ring.

Back then Jenny believed in the truth of the competition, and the wrestlers did their best to portray their matches as true sport. But now everyone knew the secret. Now, at least, Jenny knew the secret. The blood on the men that night came from cuts they made with razors they carried with them or hid under the ring. Jenny realized the

128

scars on the old man's head must have come from all the cuts he'd made to cause himself to bleed.

He had emptied his cup, so Jenny walked back over with a fresh pot of coffee in her hand. The old man saw her coming and reached into his pocket for two more B.C. Powders. After he dumped the contents into his mug, he looked up and smiled at Jenny.

"I used to watch you on TV when I was a teenager," she said as she poured his coffee. "You broke Baron Von Raschke's arm when you wrestled in Delbert once."

The man chuckled, a deep, sincere laugh. "They fined me a hundred dollars for that one, and made me pay that bastard's medical bills. Hell, he wasn't even supposed to win that match. I don't know why he didn't just let go." He stirred the powder and coffee, and reached into his vest pocket for two more powder packets. "I guess we all got carried away at times. That's why I have to eat these B.C. Powders like they're candy."

"Do those things really work? I remember seeing them advertised on TV."

"Not really. Not for the kind of pain I have. Morphine's the best. But they sponsor our matches, so we get them free. If you take enough of them, they help."

"Mr. King, are you sure you don't want any breakfast?" Jenny asked.

As he reached for his briefcase, he said, "Well, I was gonna just wait and have the lunch special. I hate to admit it, sweetheart, but I can't afford breakfast and lunch both today. We're wrestling at Clover Bend tonight, and I won't get paid until after the matches." While he spoke, he placed the briefcase on the table and opened it up. Inside were dozens of pictures—action photos and glamour shots of a much younger wrestler. He pulled them out. After making sure that no coffee had spilled on the table, he arranged them gingerly, setting them in order, making sure all the edges lined up properly.

"These pictures were taken back before they called me 'The King.'"

"They called you 'The Boogie Woogie Man' back then," Jenny said. Leaning over the table, she looked at the photos and shuffled them around to get a better look. His blue eyes strayed to her open neckline, and she grinned. She saw nothing wrong with giving the old man a peek. After all, he was quite a looker in those pictures, back in his younger days.

"Could I swap you a picture for my breakfast? I usually get five bucks apiece for them."

"Deal," Jenny said. "I want this one." She picked up a photo that showed the blue-eyed wrestler on the mat with a figure-four leg-lock on Austin Idol.

"Can I get three eggs with that, honey? Over easy? I been on the road since yesterday noon, and I'm starved."

"I'll see you get plenty, Handsome," Jenny said. "I bet I can help you sell some more of those pictures, too. But I think you can get ten bucks for them here. It'll be our little secret."

"I'll give you a cut, if you want," he said.

"Just leave me a nice tip. I don't expect anything from the pictures."

With a coffee pot in one hand and the picture in the other, Jenny left the table and walked back to see Glen. The old man had scrawled "The Boogie Woogie Man. Handsome Kenny King." across the top of the glossy photo in a barely legible style. She saw Glen watching her again as she approached the back counter. Jenny walked straight to him and said, "Check this out."

Glen took the photo and stared. "Has he got any more?"

"Ten bucks a piece. He's got all you'll ever want right there with him."

"Did he order any breakfast?"

"Yeah, after I bought a picture from him. He wants the special, with three eggs over easy. Load him up, Glen. I don't think he's had enough money to eat in a couple days. He said he's wrestling tonight at Clover Bend and won't get paid till the matches are over."

"He can't still be wrestling," Glen said. "He's gotta be seventy-five years old."

"Tonight at Clover Bend," Jenny said as she grabbed a fresh pot of coffee and left to make another round.

Some of the other waitresses had noticed the wrestler and wandered over to buy pictures from him. She could hear the man as he got into his act, the loud whoops and yells, and the jive talking that made him so famous.

Jenny had never met a has-been. In her thirties, with twin teen-age girls, Jenny wasn't old. But she knew how her feet and legs hurt at night after waiting tables all day. If Handsome had said the B.C. Powders really worked, she'd have bought a case of them. But as bad as she hurt, she couldn't imagine the pain endured by the old man during his years on the circuit, and to know that he was still wrestling and destitute at his age disturbed her. Retirement seemed so far away, and Jenny never thought about that time, for she always believed she had the rest of her life to get an education, to choose a new career. But now she wondered if she'd still be waiting tables when she turned sixty-five.

In high school, the guidance counselor told Jenny that her score of twenty-eight on the ACT was good enough to earn a scholarship to any school she wanted to attend. Partain was the counselor's name. Ms. Cora Partain.

She'd told Jenny to choose a career that would keep her from searching the want ads the rest of her life. Jenny didn't understand what the woman meant.

"Do you think a doctor ever looks in the classified ads for a job?" Ms. Partain asked.

But when she sent off for material from the colleges she'd selected, she learned that all the freshmen girls had to stay in the dorms. After being in the Children's Home for years, Jenny'd had her fill of dormitory-style living. With a job and a paycheck came independence. Giving up her freedom—freedom she'd waited a long time to achieve—was not an option. She'd worked for Glen Campbell at the café since she was a junior in high school. She'd saved her money judiciously, and when she graduated and left the home, just having her own place and her own bedroom—a bedroom no one could enter in the middle of the night—had been the thrill of her life. Then came her pregnancy, and the twins.

Glen rang the bell again at the back of the café, and Jenny turned to get the wrestler's breakfast. She retrieved his plate and muscled her way through the other admirers to set it on the table in front of him. The others politely scattered so the old man could eat.

"Did it ever bother you? That wrestling is fake?" Jenny asked.

The old man looked up from counting his money. As he folded bills and stuffed them in his pocket, he smiled at his pretty waitress. "You know, I been asked a lot of times, *is wrestling fake?* But I never been asked if it bothered me. These scars on my forehead ain't fake."

"But you put them there yourself," Jenny said.

"Yes. I did. I got fifteen dollars extra for every match I bled. It's a bit more now."

"But you did it to yourself. That made it fake, even if it *was* real blood."

"Do you have children?" Not waiting for her to answer, he continued, "Do they believe in Santa Claus?"

"They did when they were younger," Jenny said. "They're teenagers now."

"But at Christmas, do you still talk about what Santa Claus will bring you? Do you listen to Christmas carols about old St. Nick? I've even played Santa before. Supposed to do it again in Little Rock this year. I can't do it at Memphis. Ever body there knows who I am. The kids always fuck with my beard, trying to pull it. They think my beard is fake, and when they see it ain't, they start apologizing for being bad and begin telling me what all they want for Christmas."

Jenny laughed. She knew she had spent too much time with the man, but Glen didn't seem to care. If she hovered around her boyfriend, Archie Snell, Glen threw a fit.

"Everyone knows they's no Santa Claus," he said. "But we still accept him at Christmas. You know, the worst wrestling fans in the world are the little old ladies who still believe that wrestling is real. I've had them attack me before, after a match, as I was leaving the arena.

"But it's funny what people believe or choose to accept as the truth," he continued. "Do you believe we landed on the moon? Have you ever seen any proof of it, or did you just accept what they said? That raghead that predicted that earthquake in California, and now predicted one here?"

"That raghead, as you call him, hit the exact day of his prediction in California," Jenny said.

132

"Actually, he never predicted that California earthquake. He did predict the Mt. St. Helens eruption, though," he said. "But he missed this one. Did you know he bought up a bunch of stock in a bottled water company? I read all of this in the *Wall Street Journal* the other day. Yeah, I know. No one believes I'd read the *Journal*, but when I got the change and can find it, I still like to get a copy now and then. I read last week this Iben Browning is a millionaire now. Seems everyone stocked up on bottled water expecting the earthquakes to happen."

"But the threat of an earthquake is real," Jenny said. "Even though he missed his prediction, even if he gets rich in the process, he helped a lot of people get prepared. They say it's gonna happen. It's just a matter of time."

"But who are *They*, sweetheart?" he asked.

"I don't understand your question," Jenny said.

"We go around all the time saying, *They said this* or *They said that*. *They* are the experts, the government, the preachers, the politicians. The ones we expect to tell us the truth are the ones making a profit from our belief in them. Do you think everything *they* say is true? *They* expect you to."

"If that's the case, sir, then you're no better than they are," Jenny said. She noticed crumbs from his biscuit had fallen into his beard. He caught her glance, and flicked at his whiskers, tossing the crumbs onto his plate and across the table.

"Oh, don't worry about hurting my feelings, young lady. I've never told anyone wrestling was real. An eight year-old boy once killed his younger sister doing a pile-driver he saw me perform on television one Saturday. I didn't wrestle for years after that. I made sure that I never told a soul that wrestling was real after that happened. I am a performer, just like all the people you see on television. But I perform live, like the actors you see on Broadway. Yeah, I've been to Broadway, when I wrestled at Madison Square Garden in New York City. Been there many times. That always paid well. But it never seemed to be enough. People see me throw a punch that never connects, and a man falls writhing to the canvas. Some people yell 'Fake,' and some yell, 'Hit him again!' People believe what they want to believe, and their eyes and common sense have nothing to do with it."

A bell rang from the back of the café. Another plate of food was ready to be served.

"I'm sorry I started preaching at you like that," he said. "Sounds like we're more alike than I realize. Even you have to jump to the sound of a bell."

They both laughed. "That's a plate for Molly," Jenny said as she poured more coffee in the man's cup. "What is your real name?"

"Ferdinand," he said. Then he grinned. "Ferdinand C. Posey. And I do love to read the *Wall Street Journal*."

They both laughed out loud as she left and made her way back around the café. When she reached the back, she told Glen she was going out for a smoke. The girls smoked in the alley behind the diner, even though the customers were still allowed to smoke inside. Glen insisted.

Out back of the café, Jenny stood alone and lit her Misty. She'd never really thought of leaving Delbert. Where would she go? She took the girls to Destin, Florida, the week of the earthquake. They had stayed in a condo the twins' grandparents owned until they knew it was safe to come home. Destin would be a great place to live, but giving up earthquakes for hurricanes wasn't what she wanted, although hurricanes at least gave some advance warning.

She remembered when she was little, and she'd dreamed of cutting hair some day in a salon at a huge, fancy mall in a city like Atlanta or Orlando. She could still go to college, but what would she do with a degree? Maybe she could wait till the twins graduated high school and leave with them. But Donna and Dana would have outgrown her by then and wouldn't want her tagging along. She would be alone again and still waiting tables. Forty years old suddenly seemed close and malevolent.

When she came back in, she saw Ferdinand stepping out the front door. She walked to his table. He'd folded a ten-dollar bill and stuffed it up under his plate. Next to the plate was another photo. Across the top he had scribbled, "Jenny. You are an angel. King Ferdinand." She took the picture and the tip and placed it in her purse. Today was Friday, and Glen was frying catfish for lunch. By 11:30, the café would be crowded. She carried the dirty plate to the back, and then dumped some sugar into a pitcher to make iced tea. Over the loudspeakers of the café, she heard the radio playing "Rudolph the Red-nosed Reindeer," as she walked back to Ferdinand's table and wiped away the white powder he had spilled next to his coffee cup.

After all, life goes on, regardless of lovers, or dreams, or predictions of natural disasters. Tomorrow was another day, with bills to pay, children to feed, and customers to keep happy. She might lose it all someday, but for now, she had more important things to worry about. She poured another round of coffee, and with dreams of careers and wealth still swirling like sugarplums in her head, she walked to the back of the cafe to check the work schedule for next week.

Flying Lessons

Jake bought the little wooden box because of the beautiful wood-grain that showed vividly through the dark walnut stain. The precision-miter, dove-tail corners allowed the lid to fit down over the sides in an airtight seal that he was sure would never admit water. The man who sold it to him at the First-Monday Flea-Market in Ripley, Mississippi, claimed he had no idea what the box was.

"Those earphones are some kinda listening device. I think it was an old ham radio or something," Henry had said. "If you took all of that shit out, you could have a nice little jewelry box."

Henry said the box came from a yard sale in Tuscaloosa, Alabama. The lady who sold it to Henry was cleaning out her house and moving to the Bahamas because her husband, the director of the state mental hospital located on the campus of the University of Alabama, had recently died.

But Jake knew what the box held. He'd seen the electric shock treatments administered in the movie *One Flew Over the Cuckoo's Nest*. He knew of the mental hospital at Tuscaloosa, having read an article in *Sports Illustrated* about the oddity of a state mental institution housed on the campus of a flagship state university. He'd also read about the shock therapy treatments. They were supposed to induce a sense of tranquility in the more violent minds.

So Jake bought the Ectonustim 3 Electroconvulsive Therapy Machine for ten dollars.

Jake wondered what *tranquility* really meant, and if such a thing could be induced by an electrical shock. Karen had given him tranquility. *Tranquility*. He thought of what it was to feel tranquility. He didn't think of words, but of Karen in bed next to him, her naked body exposed, uninhibited, their love stripped and raw—*tranquility* being the desire to never leave, the opposite of *ambition* that forced them both from the warmth of the tangled sheets to pursue the bounty of the coming day. He remembered standing with her on the beach at Destin, watching the dolphins frolic in the surf as the masts of sailboats disappeared in the distance.

136

His years on the riverboat had forced him to run the rivers and byways of the intra-coastal waterway where land was always in sight. But he always wanted to go out in that emerald sea, to go beyond the horizon until all sight of land was lost. Flying for his uncle's crop-dusting service allowed him to experience a different ocean of blue, but land was always there below. He knew that further out into the Gulf there would only be deep blue water to replace the emerald waves close against the shore, and he yearned for those waves beyond, to experience the Gulf from the top, to suit up and dive beneath her surface to see what she hid below, to experience her hidden treasures, to consume all her secrets, while knowing all along she sat there, waiting for him to come to her. Perhaps that was the source of his feelings for Karen, knowing she would always be there. They had never discussed a future; he'd always just assumed the future. Maybe that was tranquility. Maybe tranquility was simply never wanting to move or leave. He never wanted to leave the beach, to wade back to shore after snorkeling in the surf; he never wanted to leave her side, and they always seemed to manage to find a couple days at a time when they could just be together. Until she married a doctor.

Or maybe tranquility could be achieved by an electrical shock.

Saturday night at Winks was always a busy time. Jake occasionally worked security there if Wink needed him. Some people called him a bouncer. He hated the word. Jake knew people who worked at bars and relished the title of *Bouncer*. They lacked the mentality for the position. Proving how tough you were by beating up on old drunks or sucker punching people too inebriated to defend themselves was not his idea of barroom security. Drunks acted like kindergarteners, and to provide effective security at a bar, you had to treat them like you were the kindergarten teacher.

Jake wondered if sometimes he put too much thought into everything he did. He was a perfectionist, and competitive, always striving to be the best. Being the best doorperson at a bar didn't mean being the biggest or baddest or toughest, although he could take care of any situation. But Jake knew that once the first punch was thrown, everyone was a loser. The enraged man tossed from a bar is likely to get a pistol and come back.

Two weeks ago Jake had walked a man to the door from Cardwell, Missouri. The man was not large, but Jake knew to take no one for granted. The friend of the man was tall, about six-six, with long muscular arms, and a quiet man who seemed oddly put-out by his friend's rudeness.

Jake asked them both to walk and then followed them to the door as the Cardwell man cursed him repeatedly. The man carried a longneck beer that Jake watched, expecting at any time for the man to hit him with it. When they got to the door, Jake told the Cardwell man he had to leave his beer inside, that the ABC regulations wouldn't allow them to sell carry-out drinks.

"I think I'll just stick this bottle right up your ass," said the Cardwell man. His friend scowled.

Jake recognized what was happening; he had seen it many times himself. Some mouth with an attitude goes to the bar with a friend he knows is tough, and his balls suddenly drop. He becomes a bad-ass and can handle anyone because his friend will never let it go that far.

"Would you like to finish drinking your beer first?" Jake asked.

The Cardwell man nearly choked. He looked at his friend, then at Jake. "Well," he said. "I might not do it tonight."

"I'd appreciate that," Jake said. "I'd look funny running around here with a bottle up my ass, not to mention it'd be uncomfortable as hell. Wink doesn't pay me enough to deal with that kinda shit. But here's what I'll do. If you and your friend will come back tomorrow in a better mood, I'll buy the first pitcher of beer."

The Cardwell man stared; his friend chuckled, then said, "Let's get outta here."

Drugs were always a problem at the bar. Seemed every two-bit thug who didn't want to work at the Darling plant sold methamphetamine or cooked the shit. The headlines of the local paper carried the news every day of another lab busted. At first, Jake had avoided the problem. He didn't mind the bar patrons making a bit of extra money. Some of them even tipped him to look the other way, although he always looked the other way. Jake's maternal grandfather ran moonshine over the West Virginia and Kentucky hillsides, and

Jake's Grandpa and Uncle Freddie had both been honchos with the local Klan, so Jake wasn't about to judge the way a man made his living. His uncle Freddie had carried more than one load of contraband up and down the Mississippi on the barges they ran down to New Orleans and along the intra-coastal to Corpus Christie and Brownsville.

Too many people were buying meth from Memphis, cutting it to the bone, and selling it to support their habits. Most of the meth bought and sold in the club consisted of a seventy to eighty percent cut of Vitablend and ground up Ephedrine tablets. He knew one guy who bragged of adding white pepper to his cut to make the shit burn like hell when snorted. If anyone around could cook the shit and sell it without someone finding the lab, they'd get rich. But no one could cook without the scent giving them away, so hiding a lab long enough to make a profit kept them from being in business for very long.

Saturday night wound down and last call was made. Jake was already emptying the trash cans full of empty longnecks and helping to clean the place as patrons paired off and left. Last call was given at 4:30. The bar closed at 5, and Jake made his final sweep at 5:30. There wasn't much to do in Delbert, but he could never understand what people saw in Wink's bar. Many times when he'd arrive at the bar Thursday night at 9:00 to begin his weekend shift, people would already be at their tables. Those same people would be there at 5:30 when he made his final sweep, forcibly expelling them, listening to them curse him as he took them by the arm and eased them towards the door. Those people would be at Wink's from open till close every Thursday, Friday, and Saturday night, every week of the year. He pitied them. As bland as the nightly grind at the bar had become for Jake, their lives must be even worse for them to spend that much time at Wink's.

Jake worked at the bar during the offseason for crop-dusting and when he was off the boats. The place soon wore on his nerves. It was easily the hardest money he had ever earned, but it was a great way to meet new women.

After chasing everyone out, they'd complete all the work and sit down for a couple drinks, unless the bartenders or other help had paired off with someone or had someone waiting for them outside.

Many times they'd go to Campbell's Café downtown. Campbell's opened at 6 and served the best breakfast in the county, or they'd go to someone's house where they'd continue the party or crawl under the sheets with the newest catch of the evening. Or, they'd laugh about the latest drunken fool who made the Wall of Shame—a bulletin board in Wink's office where handwritten notes of the drunken exploits of their customers were pinned next to pictures. The pictures were of patrons who'd made the mistake of passing out at the bar only to wake with their eyebrows shaved or their faces made up with an awful shade of rouge. If there had been a fight that night, they'd all walk out together, or even call the city marshal to drive by to make sure no one waited outside.

Just a year ago a drunk had been thrown out by Sissy Ringo. Sissy had beaten the man before dragging him out the door where Sissy put the boots to him for another five minutes. An hour later the man returned, and after entering the bar, had emptied a revolver into the crowd, killing Sissy with three bullets, and seriously wounding two others. After emptying his pistol, the man fled. He was found an hour later, running south as he followed the Union Pacific rails hoping to jump a freight train. As he pulled the empty pistol from his pocket, Sheriff Wilson Underwood shot him between the eyes.

But tonight had been uneventful. The cleanup was through, and Jake sat at the bar with Moose, Trisha, Matt, and Brenda. All held double-shots of Jack Daniels in throw away cups.

"I'm heading out to the witch's house for breakfast. Y'all are welcome to tag along if you like," Jake said.

"You just going out there to see that Chastity girl," Trisha said.

"Do you blame him?" Moose said.

"Hell no. If he'd let me, I'd go along with him. But when I got done with her, she'd want nothing to do with you, Jake," Trisha said.

Jake laughed at Trisha. A push-up bra, a low-cut shirt, and some lesbian smack earned her the best tips in the house. Jake always wondered if her bravado was real, if she'd ever even been with a woman. He knew he'd never seen her leave the bar with anyone on the occasional nights he worked there. She was the only one who hadn't paired off and gone home with someone after quitting time.

140

Even Wink was known to get laid once in a while, although it was usually with some girls he paid to come over from Memphis. The dim lights and her thin application of make-up hid the years of hard living, and the drug and spousal abuse she'd endured. But nothing had ever dimmed her personality and wit. Trisha was loved by all, and wanted by all.

"You never been down on a woman and you know it. You just like talking shit," Jake said.

"You'll never know," Trisha said. "But you better pray I never get to lick her ass, or she'll drop you like dead weight, baby."

Wink Gaskill burst through the door of the front office. "We're done here, gang. Y'all get home and get a good sleep on before tonight. We'll be busy, so rest up." Wink was in his early sixties. Stories of his brawls in the honky-tonks of northeast Arkansas would be told for years. Although at one time he stood over six feet, he barely made that mark now, and the barrel chest now hung around his pot-bellied waist. A thin, angry, scar ran from behind his left ear to the dimple that cleft his chin. A pissed-off partier had come back to the bar with a box cutter after being tossed. The man missed Wink's throat by a couple inches, and instead of taking Wink's life, he cut off the bottom half of an ear lobe and slit Wink's cheek through and through.

"The longer a man works in a bar, the shorter his life expectancy becomes," Wink loved to say, as if he enjoyed prophesying his own death. But Jake believed Wink reveled in being the exception to that rule. Wink couldn't say he'd never lost a fight, but he proudly boasted he'd walked away from every fight he'd ever been in. "That's plenty good for me, especially with as many as I've seen carried out of here on stretchers."

"That little Italian girl waiting for you out at the witch's house," Moose said to Jake. "Her Momma's Jewish."

"Yeah. She's an odd mix. That explains the nose," Jake said.

Moose laughed. "She got more nose that tits."

"I wouldn't say that, but I guess I'll go out there. They said they'd cook breakfast for all of us," Jake said.

"That's that little Moretti girl, Chastity?" Trisha said. "She's beautiful, Jake!"

Jake got off his stool and dug in his pocket for his keys. "You just stay away from her, unless I'm there to watch."

Trisha threw a wet towel at him. "You'll never know I saw her till she says goodbye." They all laughed and walked out the door together as Wink closed and locked it behind them.

***

Jake pulled into the witch's drive. Violet claimed to be part of a coven that had practiced and played with witchcraft since the late 1800s. She always loved coming into the club and showing Jake her latest ju-ju bag with a charm or spell she was using to hex someone who'd pissed her off. The ju-ju bags were usually stuffed in her bra, or tucked down into her panties. Her efforts to display them always revealed more than just her little bags of witchcraft. Jake always enjoyed the exhibition.

Violet was more excited about the shock machine than Jake. She wanted to try it immediately, but he refused to let her. "We don't even know if this thing still works, Violet. This thing could kill you."

So over a couple of weeks time, she talked him in to trying it on her old mule.

They ran an electric cord from the barn, baited the mule out of the pasture and into the corral with a bucket of corn, and then plugged in the machine and placed the wrapped electrodes behind the ears of the mule. Then they all stepped back.

As the mule stuck his nose into the bucket to eat the corn, Jake pushed the button that sent the shock to the mule's brain. All hell broke loose. The mule brayed and jumped nearly five feet high, falling back to the ground in a fit of kicking convulsions that ended with the mule dying right there in its tracks.

"I'm not digging the hole to bury that bastard. This was your idea," Jake said.

Violet laughed. "I have a spell that will bring him back. Don't worry about it."

Chastity was a close friend of Violet's. Chastity had been coming to the bar ever since she bought a fake ID at the head-shop over in Memphis. As long as the kids were at least 18 and had a fake

ID, Wink let them in, especially if they were cute. Chastity Moretti's hair was long and silky black. Her eyes were narrow around her Italian/Jewish nose that seemed her only flaw. She bitched when she got over 105 pounds, and for a girl who was only five feet tall, a good third of that weight had to be stuffed into the blouses she wore. She loved flashing Jake when she came to the bar with Violet. They both seemed to delight in teasing him, and Jake didn't mind.

After easing his truck off to the far side of the driveway, Jake parked and got out. The sun was high enough to light the area, so the bonfire that Violet had promised to dance around naked had died to ashes. But Jake could still hear voices inside the house. He walked to the door and entered.

Violet sat at the far end of the table in a loose-fitting halter and bikini briefs. Chastity sat next to her in a white robe wrapped around her tiny frame. Moose had arrived just minutes before Jake, but he was headed for the door to go home and sleep. Chastity looked up at Jake and smiled. Violet poked Chastity in the ribs and said, "I'm sleeping in the kid's room. Y'all go back to my room and let Jake get some rest." She hugged Chastity and kissed her on the lips, a gentle, sensuous kiss.

"Don't you leave before I get to talk to you, Jake," Violet said. "I have some cousins coming in from Yellville I want you to meet. They want to hire your helicopter. They should be here this morning. And you behave in my bed, Chastity. I don't want blood on my sheets."

Chastity led Jake down the cluttered hall to the far back door. She entered and stood next to the bed as she waited for the door to close. After locking the door, Jake turned to face her. She let the robe slip off her shoulders. She wore a black bustier with a black bikini laced in red. Jake began to undress as she slid under the covers.

"What did she mean about no blood on her sheets?" Jake asked.

"I'm on my period. There will be certain things we can't do tonight. Today. This morning. Fuck, whatever it is."

"We can put a towel under you."

"I promised her I wouldn't."

"Are you Italian?"

"My daddy was. My mother is Jewish. I look more like her than my father."

He slid under the covers with her and pulled her close. "I have never seen anyone who looked like you."

They kissed for a few minutes, then she pulled away from his mouth and nuzzled up close against his chest. As her thigh caressed his waist, her left hand eased down his torso. "Violet wants you to meet her cousins. I think they sell a lot of dope and guns. They're hoping to get something started over here."

"Do they have their own cook, or are they buying the shit?"

"They bought 500 acres up around Mammoth Springs that has a cave on it. They've set up a cook up there. I don't know. You know how Violet can be. She'll start telling something, then act like it's some big federal secret, and she'll wind up telling you just to make you think you're important when it didn't matter and she was gonna tell you, anyway."

"Why do they need my helicopter? It's just a crop duster."

"I don't know. Violet is so far out there with all of this witchcraft bullshit. Now these cousins of hers are coming in and their supposed to be some kind of connected to the Posse. They didn't actually buy the land—just leased it from some Skinheads in Idaho to set up a hunting club. They went to Colorado or Idaho somewhere to learn how to cook meth, but they sell a bunch of guns, too. They say that this earthquake scare has really boosted business for them."

"How's that?" Jake asked. "The earthquake never happened."

"Fear. People are afraid of what will happen if that earthquake ever does come. The ones with supplies will want to keep them. They say they're selling guns by the hundreds up through the Ozarks. Selling a bunch of them up at that Poplar Bluff Flea market in Missouri. They also swap for pot down at McAllen, Texas."

"Why does she want me to meet these guys?"

"They know your uncle, Freddie. I think he's been doing some business with them, but they want to meet you or something. I really don't know, Jake. I think they need someone to move some shit up the river. They're losing a lot of loads out on the road."

"I don't do any of that shit, and Violet knows that."

"Violet knows you been needing some extra money for a long time. She thought these guys might help."

"Every two-bit thug in Jester County is cooking and cutting and undercutting prices."

"These guys don't sell anything here. It all goes north up the river or back down south to Mexico. That's all I know, and I don't want to talk about that anymore."

"That's why you're here with me now. You're supposed to set all this up aren't you?"

"I was supposed to see if you were interested. But I am with you right now because I want you."

They lay beside each other for a while, listening to the birds beginning their morning songs outside the window as the day came alive. She was tiny, and Jake could move her with little effort. He brought her up close, and she lay her head on his chest.

"I never knew my father, never had any brothers, so I never had anyone to look out for me. I feel safe when I'm with you."

Jake lay quiet for a moment.

"I shouldn't have even mentioned it. But I've watched you at the club. You take care of people. I think you'd take care of me." She eased on top of him. "You'll take care of me. Won't you?"

"Don't fall in love with me, Chastity."

Jake moved out from under her, rolling over on his side where he could look into her eyes. "I'll take care of you. Always. But don't talk of love so easily. You don't fall in love with someone the first time you're in bed together. It takes more."

"I don't fall in love. I never said that. I just want allies."

He laughed at her. "You been hanging with Violet too long."

She kicked him under the sheets. "Then just go to sleep, you asshole."

Later that morning Violet strolled into the bedroom and woke them both. She sat down at the end of the bed and lit a cigarette. Chastity got up to use the restroom. Jake saw the time. He was ready for lunch.

"My cousins will be here tonight. They wanna come out and hang at Wink's tonight, but they were hoping you'd come here afterwards. They have some crop-dusting they want done."

"Why don't they just talk to Freddie? They pay him, and he tells me where to fly."

"They already talked to Freddie. This is a bit different, and I think it may be a bit more dangerous. Freddie said you had to agree to it, or he wouldn't ask you to do it."

"Well, what the hell are they wanting any ways?"

"I don't know. They won't tell me, and when they talk to you, me and Chastity have to leave."

Chastity strolled back into the room and crawled under the sheets. She snuggled up to Jake and lay her head down on his chest. "Are you two through?"

"You trying to run me off after I set you up? Behave girl or I'll jump in there with you both."

"I need some lunch," Jake said.

Violet laughed as she got up and walked out of the room. "I'll get started on some lunch. Y'all come out whenever you're ready."

***

That night at Wink's, Jake watched the door, waiting for Amber and Chastity to come in with her cousins from Yellville. Saturday nights were always the busiest night of the week, and a good crowd had already filled the bar. The live band were local favorites, and they knew how to work the crowd to get them to buy drinks and tip their bartenders.

Jake walked through the bar, speaking to old friends, asking strangers how they were doing. Then he saw Jenny and Karen sitting at a table.

Jenny was a waitress who had waited tables at Campbell's Café since she was in high school. She was a single mother of twin daughters with carrot-red hair and beautiful green eyes. Jenny herself was a beautiful woman, with long locks of brown hair and a toned body. She was known to flash a bit of cleavage at Campbell' Cafe, and some of the local ladies talked poorly of her. But Jake knew the difference it made in tips at the bar, and he had always respected Jenny for her independence. An orphan from the time she was thirteen, Jenny did her best to get by, and with the exception of a few gossips, the town loved her.

Karen was his past, but he hadn't been ambitious enough for her at the time. He helped her prepare for her RN boards, in essence helping her to find her husband, a doctor who could give her more. But when Karen saw him, she smiled and rose from the table, walking to him and kissing him gently on the cheek as she squeezed him tightly in her arms.

"What are you doing here? I haven't seen you in ages," Jake said.

"I bought a storefront here. I'm opening a fabric and design shop. Jenny helped me pick the place out this morning," Karen said as she looked at Jenny over her shoulder.

"Hi, Jake," Jenny said just before she sipped from her drink. Jenny always drank a tequila sunrise. Karen always drank an Absolut vodka tonic.

Jake stepped back from Karen and eyed her up and down. Her tight leather skirt revealed every angle of her body. Her thighs were still muscular and toned. She wore the Mahan boots he'd bought for her years ago. They'd heard an old Eddie Raven song titled "San Antonio Nights" where the singer had mentioned "knee-high Mahan boots and jeans." She made him buy her a pair that afternoon. Her muscular legs stuffed into the shit-kicker boots with a short leather skirt that revealed more than it covered reminded Jake of many wonderful nights before.

"Please, tell me you can dance with me tonight," she shouted into his ear over the music of the band. "Your girlfriend will just have to understand."

"Like your husband?"

Karen leaned forward to speak into his ear. "His toes have turned black from the diabetes. He's drinking himself into a grave. He won't be around long, Jake."

Jake squeezed her tight. "There is no girlfriend, and I'm sorry to hear that about your husband. I know you're ready to move on, but I know you loved him. That's what makes you the person you are."

She leaned back into his ear. "Just dance with me tonight. Please. When his time comes, I will not make the same mistake again.

I will not lose you again." Karen pulled away, kissing him on the cheek. She returned to her seat. As she picked up her cocktail for a drink, she winked at him. He felt a hard elbow in his ribs.

"Boy, you sure forgot where you were just a few hours ago," Chastity said.

"You told me you wanted an ally. I didn't think that meant we were exclusive," Jake said.

"That's alright. I'm here with Violet's cousin. They finally made it in, and they want to talk to you later. Can you come out again tonight?"

"Are you gonna crawl under the sheets with me one more time?"

"Already spoken for tonight, Jake." Chastity tossed a glance towards Karen. "Looks like you are, too."

"Karen's an old friend. We'll dance some tonight, but she's married, and she believes in everything marriage is supposed to be."

"Yeah. Sure. That's why she's out here tonight, kissing all over you."

Jake kissed Chastity on the cheek and pinched her booby as she walked away.

* * *

The night went much more quickly than other Saturday nights. Jake thought a bit about his meeting with Amber's cousins, but he spent most of his time pre-occupied with Karen. They had danced every slow dance, grinding against each other's bodies endlessly as the DJ played Nugent's marathon version of "Stranglehold." Jake knew Karen as a passionate woman, but she was also cold where matters of dollars were concerned. She'd married once for money. That night she told him, when she married again, it would be for love. Jake told her she read too many romance novels. That when we make a decision, we are forced to live with the consequences for life.

"Don't you think I know that? I'm living those consequences now. But I will be free soon," she said. "Will you at least give me a chance?"

"Yes," Jake said. "I promise."

When he looked around later, Jenny and Karen had paid their tab and left for the night. Chastity had left earlier for Violet's. Her sole purpose in coming to the bar had been to tell Jake the cousins had arrived, and perhaps to let him know she had already paired off with one of them. Seeing Karen had left him restless, and he knew the evening would never end, so he told Wink he was calling it a night. A half hour later he pulled into Violet's drive.

Jake walked up to the fire. Violet sat on the far side next to a tall, older looking gentleman. Three other men sat around the fire, laughing and drinking. Chastity sat on one man's lap, and as she saw Jake approaching the fire, she reached to remove the man's hand from between her legs.

"Hey, Jake," Violet said. "You're early."

"Club was slow tonight, so I thought I'd slip away and come on out."

"Jake, this is my Uncle Bob. These are my cousins, Robert, Kenny, and Logan."

Jake worked his way around the fire, shaking hands with the men and exchanging pleasantries.

"Chastity and me are gonna run into town and get some pizzas. We'll be back in a bit." Violet got up. 'Come on, Chastity."

Chastity kissed the man named Logan. Then she rose from his lap. "I'll be back shortly. Don't you go no where," she said to him. She walked to the car with Violet and they left.

Uncle Bob spoke first. "Freddie says you're a top notch crop-duster in that chopper."

"I'm glad he thinks so," Jake said. "I still have a lot to learn, though."

"He says he can trust you with anything."

Jake smiled. "What do you want with me?"

"Freddie says you know the river and the bottoms all the way to New Orleans. We've been bringing some things up the intra-coastal from Brownsville into New Orleans, and Freddie's gonna start hauling our barges up the river for us. We're still working on the drop points, and that doesn't concern you for now. But we need someone to get things from the barges to the final destination."

"Why not just offload it and drive it?" Jake asked.

"We want to keep everything off the highways. We've been losing a lot of shit on the roads. If we can keep everything on the river, the chances of losing a load are slim to none."

Logan spoke next. "We can offload from the barges as they are tied off at points on the river. We have a lab in a cave up in the hills, but we need a way to get the chemicals in. Freddie can sell us the anhydrous, and you can deliver it to the cave in your crop-duster. The helicopter. But we were thinking maybe you could help us with the barges, too. Do you think you could land that thing on a barge tied off in the river?"

"Fuck. I could land on a barge going down the river so long as it has enough room. I land on a flatbed trailer nearly every other day," Jake said.

"We can get the chemicals like red phosphorous and pseudoephedrine in Mexico. Walmart has started making all their Equate-brand shit down there, and we can get any chemical we want. In bulk. We just need to deliver them up the river and to the cave. Freddie said he could get the stuff up the river and you could take it in by chopper if you would."

"Why not just cook the shit down there?" Jake asked. "They gotta be better set with the police than you could ever be here."

"The police are no problem. It's getting the shit to cook with and keeping the cartels and gangs from blowing them up. If we ship the chemicals in industrial bulk, even if we get caught, it's simply a trade violation. As long as the shit is on a barge in the river, it's subject to maritime law, and no state can seize it or search it. The feds don't wanna waste time looking through thousands of pounds of beans and rice and gravel. Freddie brings in a dozen barges at a time of anhydrous for the Co-op. If we can get the shit to the cave, we can cook it, and you can fly it back out to the barges on the river."

Jake eased forward and asked Logan for a smoke. He offered him a hand-rolled joint. He lit it and leaned back. He took a long, hard drag. "Is this some of your stuff?"

"It's the best."

Jake nodded in agreement. "Are you selling it here? The weed and the blow?"

"Some. Most of the blow goes back to Mexico, right back down the river on the boats. The weed goes north up the Mississippi River, up the Arkansas and Ohio."

"That's smart, I guess," Jake said. "They could stash the shit in a barge of beans or rice and no one would ever check it. After the barge was tied off, they could sneak in at night and haul it off by motor boat."

"There you go." Kenny spoke for the first time.

"Here's the problem," Jake said. "No matter how careful you are, it's the small retail trade that gets you. Some meth-head out there gets busted and snitches, and everyone in the chain of production and distribution goes down with them."

"This is a bit different, Jake," Kenny said. "There are no small distributors. We cook the meth for the Mexicans to move through their own gangs in the states. We send it back down the river, and they distribute it. They got tunnels and shit. They can even send barges down through the Panama Canal and use mules to bring it in to California. The problem down there isn't with the federales, it's the other cartels killing off their cooks and attacking their labs. We have nothing to do with the distribution."

Jake toked on his joint. "So even if they lose a load, they still have the lab. But how you gonna keep a lab hid up here?"

"We have a cave. That's where we need you to fly the chemicals in from the barges." Logan was speaking now. "They pay us with guns and cash. These guys are shipping the stuff to the Italians at Tunica who run the casinos, and to some gangs here in the states. We move the guns, and there's more money in that than the dope. We even have a federal license for the guns. But they go off the boats on the river at Tunica and Tulsa, and on up the Mississippi for the Chicago market. That would be too much weight for the choppers."

"How much do I make?"

"Depends on the load. We'll start with taking you to the casino and setting you up in a suite. You'll win fifty thousand dollars that night, and file an amended tax form and pay taxes on it so you can claim it and use it."

"You gotta be kidding? Pay taxes on this money?" Jake leaned forward.

"The casinos help us clean it up. Freddie will help you a lot with the crop-dusting service. You'll start making a lot more money there. But an occasional trip to Tunica will put some bigger money in your pockets, and paying the taxes on it allows you to use it without worrying."

Jake had heard enough. "How soon do you need to know?"

Logan smiled. "Freddie said you'd be interested."

"I gotta think on this," Jake said. "You don't just join something like this and walk away. Before I get in, I wanna know how I can get out without going six-feet under. Y'all are involved with some dangerous people. But if I say yes, where do we start?"

"We go to Tunica next Friday. They'll keep us in food and women and chips. And we'll plan out our loads and drops. We still have some logistics to work out, but Freddie has already bought another landing strip along the river over by Osceola."

"Yeah," Jake said. "I thought he was just expanding so we could ship some rice and beans to Mexico. Now I see what that old fuck was up to."

"With your ability to land on the truck, and the new facilities at Osceola, we'll have a range that allows us to offload at different points along a two-hundred mile stretch of the Mississippi. We'll try to avoid using the same place more than needed."

"How do I get in touch with you Monday morning?" Jake asked.

Logan smiled as he handed him a card, then shook his hand. "We'll be right here, just call Violet or stop by."

Jake left before the girls returned with the food. He didn't want to watch Chastity with her new boyfriend, and he had a lot to consider. He knew he would do this. Losing Karen to a doctor was simply a decision of economics for her. Jake would never have that kind of money. Here was a chance to make up for what he lacked in education. He could use what he had and make the kind of money he needed. Karen would be a widow soon, but Jake refused to believe she would marry him and share her wealth. If he had more to offer, they could be together. He would risk everything to be with her.

Jake left the fire and walked to his truck. As he drove down the road, he tried to imagine landing his chopper on a barge floating down the river. He thought of logistics and loads and ranges. Modifications could be made to lighten up the Bell-47 even more so it could carry a larger payload. He thought of his costs and overhead and fuel. If he made enough he'd buy a new chopper. The extra money might allow him to open his own crop-dusting service, or to even buy the co-op from his uncle Freddie. He thought of the electric shock machine and wondered what Violet had done with her dead mule. The machine might help collect money owed them. He laughed at the thought. If you rigged the machine at a party and charged fifty bucks apiece on the promise the machine would either get them stoned or get them off, you'd have rednecks lining up around the block with cash in hand.

But there was a line that one crossed from which there was no return. This was something Jake would have to seriously consider. Jake hadn't been able to sleep for a week after that stupid mule had died, but he knew if he did this, the time would likely come when he'd be forced to kill or be killed. He needed to make sure he could do that.

He thought of the home he'd build for Karen, of the trips they'd take in his planes to Cancun and Cozumel, to Antigua and Rio. He knew then there was nothing he wouldn't do to share life with her.

About the Author

    C.D. Mitchell was born in Paragould, Arkansas, the oldest of 6 children and raised on a 12 acre chicken farm a stone's throw from where his mother now lives. While living on the farm he experienced milking cows, churning butter, butchering and sugar curing pork, pickling cucumbers, cooking poke salad, raising a garden and canning jams and jellies. After living a short while in Michigan and Illinois, his family returned to Arkansas where he completed high school and then attended the University of Arkansas at Fayetteville. He obtained a BSBA in finance and banking, and then went on to attend the University of Arkansas School of Law, completing requirements for his Juris Doctorate in December, 1987. In 2002 he decided to return to graduate school to follow his dream of becoming a writer. His second year at McNeese State University was interrupted when his son began treatment for leukemia at ST. Jude's Medical Center in Memphis. CD transferred to the University of Memphis and completed his MFA with concentrations in fiction and creative nonfiction. Clayton, his youngest son, has been in remission 10 years. He has another son, Clinton, and a daughter, Candice. All three of his children are married, and their spouses make a welcome and wonderful addition to the family.

Teaching has also played an important role in CD Mitchell's life. He has taught at four universities. Proud to be called a southern writer, CD takes great pleasure in writing about his home state of Arkansas, the south, and the wonderful people who live there. He also takes great pleasure in revealing their wonderful characters, as well as their many faults. His stories and essays have been published in several nationally and internationally recognized print and online journals. This is his second story collection. CD is currently working on a novel that will continue the stories of Jake and Karen, Freddie, Charlotte and Joue.